AF261154

Victims, The Virus and The Ventilator

Bradford J. Gilmore, MD

Victims, The Virus and The Ventilator

Copyright © 2023 by Bradford J. Gilmore, MD

Paperback ISBN: 978-1-63812-829-8
Ebook ISBN: 978-1-63812-830-4

All rights reserved. No part in this book may be produced and transmitted in any form or by any means, electronic, or mechanical, including photocopying, recording, or by any information storage and retrieval system, without permission in writing from the copyright owner.

The views expressed in this work are solely those of the author and do not necessarily reflect the views of the publisher. It hereby disclaims any responsibility for them.

Published by Pen Culture Solutions 10/03/2023

Pen Culture Solutions
1-888-727-7204 (USA)
1-800-950-458 (Australia)
support@penculturesolutions.com

Victims, The Virus and The Ventilator

Bradford J. Gilmore, MD

DEDICATION

I offer this book as a message of hope to all of us who have suffered or are suffering from the loss of health and life augmented by the global viral and mental health pandemics. I,also, dedicate this novel to those dealing with family crises including substance use disorders or mental health issues. Indeed, we gratefully thank the physicians, the nurses, medical technicians, EMTs/paramedics, laboratory workers, public health departments, and the pharmaceutical companies for their contributions of medications and vaccines. I am thankful for spiritual leaders inspiring courage, faith, and hope in these dark times.

Also, I am grateful for the critique and support in writing this novel by Dr. Michael Spangenberg and Alex Schwarm's advise and expertise for now and potential for converting the book into a movie or series.

CHAPTER ONE:

MOUNTING CLOUDS

◇◇

Ghosts crowd the once idyllic Italian city of Brescia in northern Italy. The coronavirus plague paralyzes the world in its clenched jaws and floats from town to town, seeking whom it may devour. In Brescia, Italy, the miasma of death becomes a mushroom cloud of murder and gloom. Songs and vendors, artisans, and tourists vacate the city of dreamers but are engulfed in the reality that escape is not at hand. Priests and medical personnel sparsely dot the landscape as casket after casket is carted out of empty cathedrals by the absent members of the congregation. Most are dead, dying, or mourning.

Masses were extinguished by the acolytes, bringing the worsening message to Italian families too afraid and exhausted to mourn. Too lonely, the isolated families purged by this frightful, death-chomping combination cannot speak and are too overwhelmed to utter a sound. Their eyes, bloodshot from weeping and fatigue, sapped of the faith that once permeated the city. Hopeless of anything, pleasant memories were clouded in dust and ash. But who can remember yesterday to face tomorrow? The Doctor reflects on his life's journey of miracle and tragedy. Survivors walking alongside victims.

Luca Vitali was born in September of 1956 into an impoverished but large extended Roman Catholic family in the small North Italian town of Travaglia. He was the oldest of seven and was often asked to run and do errands. His father was often incarcerated while Luca grew up, so he raised their family with his mom. This young man longed to find a missing father or brother that would fill in their absence. He could never fill that black hole and void inside, but it consumed him Hourly and daily from birth to the grave.

At fourteen, Luca met Primo Rossi during one of his excursions to Piovere Di Tignale. Luca's bicycle chain had jammed, and he was attempting to fix it on the side of the road. The day was unbearably hot and muggy. Mirages were only steam ascending and oscillating off the pavement from the exhaust of cars passing by. The sun was intense, and sweat poured down Luca's neck. So much so that Luca and the townspeople could only hope and pray that clouds would move in to block the beastly sun.

Luca had been sitting on the side of the road, working on his bike fruitlessly. Finally, he strained up and started walking with stinging blisters on his right foot that stung with every step. The lad headed down the road limping, using his unwieldy bike as a crutch. He executed great strength to keep from falling on the pavement or plunging deep into the culverts on either side of the road. He headed down the middle of the highway as best he could with his bike in hand. His home lay miles ahead.

However, ruinous thunderheads rolled in thicker and darker until nearly pitch-black. A darkness that Luca felt. Then it began storming. It had been a scorching day, so every raindrop felt heaven-sent. Looking up to heaven, he said, "Thanks, God. Water at last! Now I've got to get home quickly! Please send help. I got to get home! In Nomine Patris et Filii et Spiritus Sancti. Amen." He crossed himself as a religious Roman Catholic, then ambled toward his home about 7 miles ahead.

The wind howled as if a ravaging wolf was descending to eat him. The gale made each step almost as fruitless as it had been with his bicycle. The gusts of wind were staggering. The raindrops, which started as plump spots of rain on the street, changed into torrents of flooding water. There was no hiding place, and Luca wondered if cars would see him. Falling into the ditch would mean devastating peril; no one might find him for days. Lightning struck nearby. One bolt fractured a tree branch off within ten feet of the young man. There was no hiding place from the storm, and small hail rattled against his head, arms, chest, and legs. It was challenging to walk unimpededly.

Unexpectedly, Primo Rossi, a twenty-something-year-old, went speeding by but caught a glimpse of Luca walking his bike in the downpour. He screeched out a U-turn and then drove up to Luca. "Hey, buddy, are you going somewhere?" Primo asked. "Pretty nasty weather, huh? Can we give you a lift?"

Caught off guard, Luca yelled, "What did you say? Oh. Sure!" The rain started pelting him harder and harder. So, Luca raced to the car with his bike in hand as best he could. The road was silvery and blurred by the storm. Thunderclouds were monstrous and threatening. As another lightning bolt hit the skies, Primo and his friend, Hannah, exited the car and opened the trunk. They shoved Luca's bike on some old rags. The half-opened picnic basket was in the backseat, where Luca was ready to climb in and sit. But Hannah made it there before he did. All tucked safely in the car, they sped off to Brescia.

He got into the car and said, "Thanks for giving me a ride back to my place. That is very kind of you. My name is Luca Vitali. I live up in and go to school in Brescia. How about you? Where do you live?"

Primo piped up, "Hi! My name is Primo Rossi. That's Hannah. She's from Germany. I am originally from Florence but now attend the University of Bologna."

"What are you studying there?" Luca queried.

What started as an everyday conversation evolved into a deep, almost mystic conversation between Primo and Luca. They talked like they had been friends for years. Unlike Luca, Primo came from a wealthy, aristocratic background and lived in Florence. Primo attended the finest institutions of higher learning. Instead of a professional degree in medicine or law, he explored being a zoologist or microbiologist.

Hannah yawned dramatically to quench the young men's conversation, but the guys ignored her. She sighed heavily and loudly and said, "Shut the hell up! Why don't you talk to me? "To her dismay, Primo and Luca were considering their differences. They contrasted people with low incomes with the well-to-do life of privilege together with Luca's perpetual experience of want.

Primo answered, "My mom wants me to study medicine or the law, but my passions lie elsewhere. I love biology, especially microbiological research. We should all be concerned as the world gets closer and closer. Some undiscovered viruses or bacteria will be trafficked worldwide by travel. I do not want so much to treat patients one by one day in and day out. Yet my passion persists. I want to find and track new and serious bacterial or viral infections and outbursts of disease. In a sense, I want to be a Sherlock Holmes of the invisible micro-world and follow the clues to solve its mystery. I want to be the one who develops the vaccine or medicine to stop the germ in its tracks. My university influences medicine, science, world policymaking, and international public health. That suits me just fine."

Luca smiled and said, "That sounds amazing. I wish you the best in that noble dream. I am only fourteen, yet I will be somebody one day. I just know I will! I love playing football [soccer], and some think I am pretty good for my age. That would be a fun life," Luca told Primo with a heartwarming grin. "I am a pretty good student, too, and get good marks, but I don't know if I will ever get into a university... I certainly couldn't pay for it. I dream of traveling outside Italy and seeing the world, but I could never afford it. Besides, I have six siblings and a mom to care for."

Primo said, "I don't know what it is like to have brothers and sisters. I am an only child. My mom was too old to have another baby safely, and my dad died from cancer before I was born. So, my uncle took us in. He has been like a father to me."

"So, your dad is dead? I'm so sorry to hear that! It's too bad you had to grow up with no brothers and sisters. Sorry for the loss of your father. Did you have any cousins to be with when you moved into your uncle's space?" Luca asked in a concerned voice.

"No, it was just my mom, uncle, and me. My dad died before I was born. But we did have a nice place outside of Florence, where I grew up. Although my uncle was rich, he seemed to need more and more to satisfy him. He was always after me about this or that. I was happy to leave there when I did. I haven't returned home since I started college a year and a half ago," Primo said.

"I am the oldest kid in our family, so I do most of the chores and find ways to help my mom make ends meet. My dad, well, my dad is a convict and almost a political prisoner because of his socialist views and abandoned Benito Mussolini and the fascist regime during WWII.

He has been off and on in prison for as long as I can remember. So yeah, it's pretty shitty that we both grew up without our dads. I'm glad your uncle that at least you had someone besides your mom when you grew up."

Luca took his gaze off Primo and looked hauntingly out the rainswept window, holding back a tear or two in both eyes. He had always wanted to talk with someone openly. Luca wanted someone like an older brother to chat with or his dad. Some man with whom he could trust and confide. He had thought the priests would somehow magically satisfy that void. They did not. They could not span the chasm between Luca's dreams and his reality.

Also, being a religious boy, he felt alone in an unsettling way. The need for a father's embrace or a pat on the shoulder to encourage Luca was all he needed. Was it wrong to want some stranger like Primo to fill those shoes? When his dad returned periodically before and after he was incarcerated, he was always angry, battered him and his mother, but rarely his siblings, and drank until he blacked out. Luca didn't want him to be his father. A stranger would be better than that, he mused.

"Luca, are you OK?" Primo asked.

"Primo, I'm OK. I sometimes just get lost in my thoughts. I daydream a lot. That's all. I can't wait to go to a university if some miracle happens.

Meet new people. Study something fancy like you are doing. Breathe some fresh air. It's so claustrophobic and constricted where I live!" Luca exclaimed. "Breaking free is as unlikely as brushing hens' teeth!" They both chuckled.

Primo put his hand on Luca's shoulder and said, "You will. I am sure of it! You will do something that the world so far hasn't done. Something amazing. Maybe, like me, you will go into virology or infectious disease. Something like that. I don't know why I am saying this since we just met, but you will be what I call a light-catcher. You will discover or do something wonderful no one has even thought of. In your way, you will be a hero." Luca crunched his eyebrows together in disbelief and doubt. No one, I mean, no one, had been in his corner before and was rooting for him. That shockingly provoked his desire to stay with Primo and talk more.

Breaking up the clouds allowed a narrow ray of sun to fall on Luca's home, and the rain let up. Luca looked up as Primo passed his small, dingy house. "Whoa, we just passed my place!" Primo again did his famous screeching U-turn, splashing the curbside, and returned Luca to his place. Both boys hopped out of the car and retrieved Luca's broken bike. After getting his possession, Luca stood motionless and gazed wide-eyed at Primo. Primo was a bit startled by his passenger's appearance. Luca Vitali was only fourteen but matured quickly, sexually and intellectually. Thick, wet, black, curly hair donned his brow and curled over his collar. He could find his darkly tanned face beaming from outdoor work in Brescia and surrounding towns. Likewise, his mahogany skin was tight; his shoulders were broad with chest, arms, and leg muscles that were athletic in keeping with his beauty. He had a soft, stubbly beard, which was filling in. His mustache was jet-black yet still thin and juvenile. However, Luca's eyes were the most impressive and attractive to Primo. They were deep-set and doleful but penetrating. Luca's azure gaze was stunning. He hesitated, and there was a long silence between them. It was the most extended silence during the trip. Primo sighed, gave Luca a big manly hug, and quickly stepped away. Luca was startled and a bit confused. He felt a gut reaction and attraction to his driver but uttered no sound and remained motionless.

Primo stepped forward again and said, "Luca, I want to stay in contact with you and see how you're doing. Maybe?" He pulled out a pen and store receipt and wrote down his name, address, and telephone number. Tearing off a section of the paper, Primo handed the pen and requested Luca's address and phone number, which he readily gave. Primo was attracted to him, but he was just a kid. Maybe a new friend. That's all. Primo and Luca would meet again. As he had done, Primo would come into his life at the most unlikely moments as if he were an apparition, a ghost. Maybe even an angel? Again, Primo would almost poetically pull Luca out of the tragic storms ahead and repair the brokenness to see Luca in a safe place.

However, resilience qualified him for the tragedies and near escapes ahead. Even as a youngster, Luca's nature relentlessly and clearly showed through his perseverance and ability to take hard punches, qualifying him for calamities and close calls. He would stand against bullies on the school grounds, defending the innocent even if it meant a black eye (or two), bloody nose, or broken ribs, and as a physician, he took on the guff that came his way. The question of resolve, toughness, and buoyancy will be tested in the future, wave after wave of pandemics, sometimes shipwrecking himself and his family. Sometimes, there would need to be more life preservers than there were.

Luca had no big brother to confide in for sexual information or life direction as the oldest child of seven. He would stand against bullies on the school grounds, defending the vulnerable, risking himself instead of them having to do it. Irresistibly good-looking from birth, he also possessed a genuine benevolent and generous character. In school, his intelligence and quick wit were unmistakable. At the same time, he was competitive in both study and athletics—an outstanding football (soccer) player and track and field star.

Moreover, he devoted himself to social justice. For example, he would forcibly advocate when another student was reprimanded or disciplined harshly and unfairly by a schoolteacher, a coach, or other disciplinarians. This behavior, of course, was not without its risks and repercussions.

His blue eyes were large but woeful beyond their years. His dimpled cheeks were rosy and round. He had aquiline nasal features. Dark brown skin covered his sculpted muscles and brawn, left to the sun and sky elements during work and play. His ivory-white teeth graced his face. He had sharp jawlines and a noticeable Adam's apple. And fleshy despite growing up without a lot of food. So, his concave, muscled belly was to be expected. He made friends effortlessly with his striking good looks, compassion, brilliance, and sense of justness. That was, of course, unless social bias would disembowel such magnetism. As he matured from adolescence through adulthood, this predisposition was his lot. Because of his attractiveness, he had sometimes fought off sexual and romantic advances from girls and boys, women and men alike.

Like many fourteen-year-olds from a strong religious background, his sexuality was tempered with curiosity, confusion, and calamity. Handsome, young, and inexperienced, he had felt attracted to Primo and even desirous of him. His Roman Catholic faith would survive, though it often met with strong opposition, despite dissent and belittlement from his friends, schoolmates, and colleagues.

From an early age, he would assist his mother in caring for his maternal grandmother. Unfortunately, she was disabled from rheumatic heart disease, later dying from congestive heart failure and influenza. On his fifteenth birthday, he refused to nurse his grandma that day and snuck out with his first girlfriend, Angelina Roncalli, for his first sweetheart kiss. It was a lackluster kiss and blackened by the taste of her cigarette-tainted breath. Both thought, "What's so damn special about this, anyway?"

CHAPTER TWO:

SHATTERING THE NATIVITY

◇◇◇

Defend You in Each Battle

If I could defend you in each battle
The first thing that I'd do
Is guard and keep watch for every moon,
sunrise, and sunset. too
'til eternity passes away
Joined hand-in-hand` with you

Our love makes days last forever
and shapes our dreams to come true
I'd store each night in a treasure box
Again, I would spend them with you

But there never seems to be enough time
To do the things you want to do
Search them out and find them
I've inspected streets and lanes enough to know
That you're that I want to know
That you're the one I want to go

Through time with

If I had a safe with lock and key,
just for whispered wishes
And wonders that had yet to come true
The safe would be empty
Except for the memories
and the melody of

But there will never be enough time
To say the things I want to say
Once on my tongue, they wouldn't stay
I've searched high and low for you
that's enough, and I know
That you're the one I want to go
Through time with

Bradford Gilmore (AgapePhileoEros) 2023

(Loosely inspired by "Time in a Bottle" Songwriter: Jim Croce)

Although very much intent on their professional careers, Luca and Anna-Claire enjoyed their growing family at home and their extended family's comfort in other northern Italian towns. They relied on family instead of daycare facilities (prevalent in the United States) to help their children's upbringing. Admiration for people experiencing poverty was second nature to them, and despite later fame and privilege, both had and maintained many indigent friendships with whom they had grown up.

Again, Anna-Claire was pregnant with her second child, Giuseppe. As the pregnancy progressed, she ended up doting on Giovanni. While he played with his toy trucks and blocks, the only toys his parents could afford, she would be in the room humming songs that her mother used to sing to her growing up. She loved being a mom. Despite sharing only scanty material wealth and the decreasing time they had to spend with each other, she adored Luca. The beginning of her second gestation was smooth as silk, and her nausea with Giuseppe was minimal and short-lived compared to what she had with Giovanni. Everything was progressing as planned; her "due date" was January 3, 1980.

Vani was aglow with thoughts of Christmas and the promise of his first Lego set. All his neighborhood friends already had them, which irritated him, but this year, it was Giovanni's turn; it was as if he were a teenager waiting for his sixteenth birthday to drive a car! A mark of maturity and "a class distinction" over the cheap wooden blocks given to him by his Aunt Aria, who bought them last Christmas for him. In fact, the family had to pull together to scrape up all the loose change to purchase anything this year.

Although Anna-Claire went to the university part-time to study environmental science, she cherished the time she spent with Vani, playing with blocks and reading children's books to him. Both told Vani about having an exceptional Christmas present this year and tried to stir some enthusiasm and acceptance about having a baby brother to play with after the expected delivery in a few weeks. That never appeared to get through to him, and there was no excitement about being a big brother. In fact, "What is a big brother and so fun about that? No, thanks! I am fine with being the only kid in the family. No intruders" was Vani's unverbalized thought.

Luca could pick up a small income by taking medical school lecture notes, distributing them for a small fee, and assisting his fellow residents with labor-intensive procedures in the understaffed newborn intensive care unit. At that time, becoming a neonatologist or a pediatric infectious disease specialist was foremost in his mind. He and his colleagues were pelted during this Yuletide with many high-risk newborns with rare and complex illnesses or others more common but labor-intensive. Typical procedures like intubating, establishing intra-umbilical IVs, chest tube placement, and exchange transfusions for hemolytic anemia or high levels of bilirubin) were more frequent. Also, congenital disabilities seemed to happen more this Christmas season.

A few residents came in sick with influenza with its accompanying cough and sore throat. They worked because of the staffing shortage and the complexity of newborn illnesses this season. Because the season was so intense, the physicians performed more often and efficiently. Finally, Christmas Eve came, and it was time for a much-needed break for Luca to enjoy the holidays with his family without interruption.

But just before leaving for home on December 20, Luca received an urgent call from home. It was Anna-Claire. "Hi, darling. Vani and I have a deep cough and sore throat. The Doctor thought it was strep throat, so he started us on some Amoxicillin yesterday. When I had one of these coughing spells, it looked like I passed my mucus plug, and then my water broke. The plug didn't seem like the one I passed with Giovanni. It was a gray-green color and slimy. I immediately called the new obstetrician, Dr. Yang, and she was concerned something was wrong, too. She asked me if the baby had been moving with his usual activity over the last couple of weeks. I realized our baby had not been moving; I hadn't felt him much over the last two to three weeks. She wants me to come in immediately for a newborn stress test and monitoring. Can you come home quickly…like right now and get me there, pick up Giovanni, and get him to one of his aunts to stay while we investigate what's going on?" she demanded urgently.

"Yeah, sure enough. I'll come home as fast as I can. I was going out the door when you called. Also, I should be home within 10-15 minutes," exclaimed Dr. Luca Vitali. Dr. Vitali hurried to his old car and prayed it would start promptly. The car was nearly on its last leg but was still drivable. He hopped in and thanked God; it began with one critical turn. Something was working! Perhaps it was a good sign that everyone would be OK, and we could all make it home by Christmas Day with a warm and relaxing celebration. That should be possible, but something else must be wrong.

But in the pit of his stomach, Luca felt an awful, eerie dread he had never had before. His mind was clouded with nearly every neonate he labored over to keep their parents and families from grief. Generally, he had been successful in that aim. One regret was that his good friend, Galen Moskos, who came from a small Jewish community in northwestern Greece before migrating to Bologna, lost his newborn son two weeks earlier. Paradoxically, Galen was in a pediatric neurology fellowship when his son died from a massive cerebral hemorrhage. Anna-Claire attended the Moskos's boy's funeral and burial. She saw first-hand the grief of losing a child in the Romaniote Jewish family. The men ripped and tore their shirts in mourning, and loud wailing followed. The ability to grieve demonstrably, like Galen's family and the community, helps have traditions that have helped generation after generation. It was a sight that Anna-Claire had never seen. It shook her inside and out; she couldn't control her tears when she told Luca about it.

Believe it or not, Dr. Vitali heard that morning he was offered a neonatology training and position in Milan because of his skill, swift discernment of young babies' diagnoses, ability to comprehend the whole picture, and ability to rapidly apply corrective measures and cures. He was known as a physician with a 'golden touch.'Hopefully, that touch will be as effective with his own children. Before Anna-Claire's call, Luca was apt to say "yes" to the opportunity, but he would discuss the prospect with Anna-Claire over the holiday week they intended to have.

Meanwhile, his wife quickly bathed and dressed Vani. She bagged his toiletries, diapers, crayons, coloring books, children's storybooks, and Aesop's fables. And a few pieces of fruit he loved. Aria arrived within a moment, came to Anna-Claire's and Luca's home, and distracted Vani by playing with his wooden blocks and watching his favorite cartoons. Dr. Vitali rushed home, picked up Anna-Claire, and relied on Aria for Vani's care.

Quickly, the Vitalis made it to the obstetrical suite. Vani had a constant runny, snotty nose but otherwise looked OK. The nurses and Dr. Yang immediately escorted Anna to get examined and tested for fetal distress. The newborn stress test demonstrated that the baby was in trouble; he had profound heart rate deceleration, worsened by his mom's coughing jags and contractions.

An emergent Caesarion section was urged. Then, Anna-Claire was prepped for surgery while Dr. Vitali dressed in scrubs to watch his child's birth and his wife's delivery to see if their newborn son had any distress.

Speedily, Anna-Claire got her sedation and anesthesia. Almost the moment she was under its effects, Dr. Yang opened her up, and the baby was delivered expeditiously.

But then there was an intercom page for Dr. Angelini, who got to the room within seconds. Dr. Vitali and he were the only people available for the immediate care of Giuseppe. No other nurses. No other physicians. No. Not a one. It was left up to Dr. Angelini and Giuseppe's father to save his life. Almost automatically, these two men labored with the Doctor's son. Giuseppe was blue and not responding to tactile stimuli. He had a heartbeat, but it was slow for a newborn. The baby did not grimace or cry but had some flexion. His son was not limp, but his joints were fixed in flexion. Therefore, his APGAR (neonatal assessment looking at color, heart rate, reflex irritability, and breathing in newborns with 0-10 scores) was 2 at one minute. Rapid measures needed to be performed skillfully, confidently, and swiftly if Giuseppe would survive.

Dr. Angelini intubated and got him on a ventilator with high settings. Immediately. Dr. Vitali put two IVs and arterial lines to give fluids and medicines through the umbilical stump and raised Giuseppe's blood pressure and heart rate. By five minutes, the APGAR got up to 5. It was going to be touch-and-go over the next 72 hours.

After Luca did his part, he dropped to the ground, sobbing uncontrollably and inconsolably. Dr. Angelini said, "Dr. Vitali, we should have your son transported to a better and well-staffed NICU across town to receive the best care possible." Luca gave the nod for the transfer. Meanwhile, Anna-Claire was awakening from deep anesthesia-induced sleep and sedation. She didn't know what was happening in the adjacent room with Giuseppe and Luca.

Meanwhile, Aria and Giovanni kept playing and watching cartoons, but she had to work in the morning, and it was getting late. It was obvious that Giuseppe needed to be on life-support in an excellent tertiary care NICU. This Christmas would not be a fun one, but one to remember. Hopefully, conditions will change for the better. Dr. Vitali kept muttering about his imperfections and why Giuseppe was in so much trouble. "What-ifs" flooded his mind. He spent the rest of the night in prayer. The following day, to his joyful surprise, Giuseppe had not died. Instead, he showed some signs of improvement. His kidneys and liver tests were improving, and his color returned to pale but fleshy, pink skin. However, he only had minimal movement. Nevertheless, he and his mom felt some relief. But Luca was trapped in a three-ring circus, like a juggler with too many balls to catch on stage and keep in motion.

After Luca regained his composure, he called to speak with Aria. "Hello, Aria, this is Luca. How are you doing? How is Vani? Is he sleeping, or may I talk to him?" asked Luca. In the background, he could hear Vani crying, and Aria answered, "He hasn't eaten much and, for the most part, been quiet and seems restless. Vani clung to me more than usual and just picked at his food. He keeps on calling for you and Anna. How is everything with you guys? Is Anna-Claire alright? How is the baby doing? I think Vani needs one of you to talk and hold him to reassure himself that you are OK."

Giovanni came to the phone immediately when he recognized Luca's voice. "Papa. Papa, come home with Mommy!"Luca greeted him in his toddler way. "How are you, my big boy? We'll be home as soon as we can. Mommy's getting better after your baby brother was born. His name is Giuseppe, and he's pretty sick, so I won't see you tonight, but I promise I will tomorrow, OK?" Luca said warmly and softly." You play with your Auntie Aria now. We will be home with a giant Christmas present. We will have some fun soon. OK?"

Vani whimpered, "OK, Papa. Bye-bye." he pulled away from the phone and returned to his wooden building blocks. He attempted to build a house with Aria's help. "How are Anne-Claire and Giuseppe?" Aria reiterated. "You don't sound thrilled. What's wrong, Luca?"

Dr. Vitali said," I will tell you more when Vani isn't around the phone." Aria left Vani in the other room but kept her eye on the young boy. Cupping her hand over her mouth, she whispered, "Tell me more."

Luca stated, "Anna-Claire is recovering from an emergency C-section because Giuseppe is ill, very ill, and on a ventilator. I don't know how he'll do in the long run, but he has shown modest improvement in the last few hours. Keep on praying. It will be touch and go for the next few days. But I will keep my promise to Giovanni and spend some time with him tomorrow."

During Giuseppe's time in the NICU, Luca went to the priests and prayed with them repeatedly. He got some relief from his troubles and could function. Anna-Claire was quite sore but otherwise doing well medically. The next day would be Christmas Eve. Fortunately, before the obstetrical problems, Luca bought the promised big present Vani had been waiting for--Legos! He had laid the box of them unwrapped in the back seat of his old automobile.

Anna-Claire was anxious to see her newborn and be released to go home to Luca and Vani and to get out of the hospital. Obviously, the number one goal was to see her newborn son with Luca. Also, she missed Vani and yearned to be home before Christmas. After waiting another hour for her husband, she got antsy and annoyed. Luca should have responded to her call by now., It was unlike him to ignore or put her off for a long time... She had all of her belongings and medicine.

. "Excuse me. Could someone watch my stuff, please? I would like to see my son., Giuseppe Vitali, in the NICU." One of the male nurses came from the nurses' station to Anna-Claire's room to accompany her to the unit. She asked, "Have you seen my husband around this morning?"

The nurse said, "Yes, we saw him a bit ago. He wanted to meet you in the NICU. We heard from him when you were released and talked to Dr. Yang. I will walk with you. Here is a wheelchair we can use to get you there. Walking the distance might aggravate your pain from surgery." he knew something was amiss but wouldn't tell Anna-Claire anything more.

Finally, they reached the NICU and saw her husband speaking with the group of doctors. "Hey, Luca. Over here!" she called. Dr. Vitali looked up to see her but looked despondent and exhausted. She picked up on the tension in the atmosphere. The feeling of dread was palpable.

Dr. Vitali left his colleagues to give his attention to his wife and bring her to Giuseppe. Luca noticed a familiar face in the NICU medical consultants as she walked over. It was Galen Moskos, the pediatric neurology fellow. Anna-Claire had attended his son's funeral and deeply empathized with Galen and Angelica Moskos.

Luca trudged over to his wife with the worst news he had ever had, and he didn't know how to soften the blow. "Hi, honey. I have some terrible news that Galen and the other attending doctors told me. Giuseppe started having seizures. They haven't been able to stop them with any medicine; also, they said he has massive bleeding in his brain. The swelling and pressure in his brain cannot be stopped with either mannitol or phenobarbital-induced coma. These drugs would have worked by now if they were going to. We could keep him on the ventilator, but we are only postponing the inevitable. You and I must decide whether to keep him on or take him off life support. Once he is off, he should sadly die pretty quickly. We should call the priest and baptize him before taking him off."

Anna-Claire and Luca burst into tears, and she became light-headed, but the male nurse who brought her from OB caught her and put her back in the wheelchair. The priest baptized Giuseppe "in the Name of the Father, the Son, and the Holy Spirit. Amen." But when Giuseppe came off mechanical ventilation, he did not die immediately. After waiting an hour, he was still with agonal breathing, albeit very slowly. The temptation was to put him back on the machine. But after talking to Galen, they moved him with his parents to a small "Christmas suite" adjacent to the NICU where they could have time with him as he died. Hour after Hour, Giuseppe was cradled in the arms of family members, primarily by his parents. Anita and Romeo, and when Aria arrived, she held him, too. Without Anna-Claire's or Luca's consent, Aria brought four-year-old Vani. Vani did feel somewhat intimidated but scurried over to his parents and then to Giuseppe to give them his pecks of kisses. He did not cry, but he was quiet and behaved. Their newborn died precisely at 22:00 (10:00PM) on Christmas Eve (1981).

When he passed, everyone felt the most bitter cold they had ever felt; it was like having ice-cold blood. The burial took place two days later, and until then, no one talked much, including young Vani. When it was time to put the baby in the ground, Vani stood in the way of the casket as if to say, "Nobody's putting my brother anywhere." That same boldness and protectiveness, even as a young soul, he carried with him—much like his father. He had severe brush-ins with his family but was resolute, courageous, and daring as circumstances involving the Vitali family and name emerged. Luca called it "Stubborn love!"

After Giuseppe's death, his parents had difficulty focusing on something besides him. The first month was the hardest to get through. Although Anna's parents and Luca's mother had died before this tragedy, there was not the exploding grief that the couple was experiencing now. The intensity of emotion lessened with time but came in waves of suffering; the loss of Giuseppe was permanent. Future Christmases and the holidays brought thoughts of this year's tragedy.

Within a few weeks, Luca and Anna-Claire doubled their attention on Vani. Playing LEGOS was the best time for the family of three. The hour after every dinner was cherished family time., but about 50% of the time, Dr. Vitali was late for dinner and talk time afterward. Nonetheless, an intimate bond between the three was secure…rock solid!. At home, Anna-Claire was the center; in her unique, benevolent way, Vani and Luca's family activity revolved like spokes on a wheel under her direction.

Anna-Claire asked, "Vani, what do you want to be growing up? "Mama, I don't know," Vani replied. "I want to be like you and Papa. Maybe I want to be a fireman and save people from burning buildings and go into a house on fire and save people. Or put people back together in an ambulance and then go fast to the hospital."

"That sounds terrific, Vani. Helping people in trouble shows you love them. You are a courageous boy! Only some people are brave enough to face fire without fear to rescue someone besides themselves. But you are special, an extraordinary boy," Anna-Claire reached over and squeezed her schoolboy tightly and kissed his forehead. "Your Papa and I love you so much. Papa rescues people, too, but not running through burning buildings. Your Papa is a hero, too. He is courageous to help people.. Papa is a healer. His middle name is "Chiron," a "wounded healer" Vani. Do you promise that you will help your Papa when he needs it? Always respect him. He is a good man. He loves you very much and will help you. Stay on the path of love and hope."

"I will, Mama, I promise. I love you, Mama! I love Papa, too!" Vani exclaimed. "I promise." That commitment will be tested repeatedly on those rough roads and spiral journeys ahead.

CHAPTER THREE:

DISASTER IN DEEP WATERS

◇◇

Six months after Giuseppe's funeral, ordinary life slowly began re-emerging. Luca was back to his overwhelming burden of work and crowded schedules, and Anna-Claire was back to being a part-time student in ecology and the environment. Vani matured quickly after his brother's death as a newborn, and within a few months, he started his primary education. Anna-Claire became involved with Giovanni's schooling and became his chief advocate, even in small things. Mother and son were nearly inseparable. Vani grew accustomed to being in the limelight and relished being an only child with its perks of being alone with his parents and the joy of one-on-one conversations--being a close-knit family was treasured by all three.

Nevertheless, Luca and Anna yearned to have an additional member or two in their nuclear family. Although with some trepidation, because of the loss of Giuseppe, Luca and Anna-Claire decided to have another child. When there was a space in time and schedule for the two of them to be alone together, they made love often and enjoyed a cup of coffee with one another early in the morning and prayers in the evening. Mealtimes at the Vitali home had special significance since Giuseppe died. Sitting together was a pillar of strength when times got rough and one of joy when good news was in the air. They needed to preserve a happy home where all three could share freely and intimately talk, mainly when discussing stressful and required hidden situations. Despite Dr. Vitali's busy schedule, Luca, Anna-Claire, and Vani were buddies and pals and were a family. There is no hierarchy, just love and respect on a level plane.

However, Anna-Claire's third pregnancy with an additional son was difficult. The pregnancy brought nausea and vomiting more than she had with either of her first two. She became anemic and had gestational diabetes at six months. Vani recently turned six, and he wanted the same participation of his mother in school activities as he had before the pregnancy. That included coming to his football (soccer) games. He didn't like the fact of becoming an older brother. He was intensely verbal against having a new sibling. Not at all! Indeed, he didn't want anybody that made his mother so ill. If that baby was doing it, get rid of it. He thought my best friend (Anna-Claire) was being consumed by having another child. Will this be another Giuseppe and all the commotion that followed his birth?

His mind was full of spite and anger. Around St. Francis of Assisi's (the patron saint of Italy) Day, October 4, he blurted out when he saw his mom vomiting and weak, "I hate my brother! I hate him! I hope he dies just like Giuseppe!" Anna was too sick and weak to respond to that statement, but she did hear him curse the pregnancy and the little fellow inside. That wounded her deeply.

Luca came home late as Anna-Claire prepared Giovanni for La Vigilia and Mass on Christmas Eve. As dark blood streamed down her thighs and legs, Anna-Claire shrieked in shock and stabbing pain.

Panicking six-year-old Giovanni saw Luca come through the backdoor and darted to his Papa. Shouting as he ran, "Papa, papa…come, help Mommy! Help!" Grabbing his dad's fingers, Vani pulled him to the stairs, where Anna was bent forward with her hands on her tummy, moaning loudly. Luca knelt, looked at Anna with woeful eyes of concern and compassion, and spoke. "It's going to be OK, honey. Let's get you to the hospital right now."

Luca picked up the phone and dialed an emergency call. "Ciao, this is Dr. Luca Vitali. My wife needs an ambulance immediately! Immediately. Hurry! Address: 110 Via Oslavia here in Bologna. She is pregnant. Her water broke and was full of blood. Abruptio placentae, I believe. Her pulse is 104, and she is drenched in a cold sweat and very pale. Shock is setting in! Hurry! Her Doctor is Dr. Monica Romani. Her hospital is Azienda Ospedaliero-Universitaria Policlinico Sant'Orsola Malpighi. Notify surgery, STAT!"

At last, they arrived, got Anna on the cart, and then the ambulance shot into the dark with flashing sirens and lights. With Vani crying, sitting in the corner with knees covering his face, Luca sighed, gathered him, and hurried them off to his cousin, Anita, and her husband, Romeo, who lived a block down the street.

Luca arrived at the hospital—pasty, clammy, and winded. In the Emergency Department, a doctor and colleague, Nick DeLorenzo, met briefly with him. Nick explained, "We sent her immediately to the Obstetric OR. Anna-Claire was typed, crossed, and started on blood transfusions, platelets, and FFP. She had abruptio placentae, as Luca had predicted, but she had disseminated intravascular coagulopathy [DIC) with her blood clotting and bleeding simultaneously; also, it will be touch and go for a little while. Fortunately, your son appears to be hanging in there, though. Thank God you made it home when you did!"

"Thanks, Nick. I've got to sit down for a second. Where can I grab something to eat, a candy bar or something, and some coffee? With the holiday and all, I haven't had time to eat today...." Dr. Vitali stated.

Dr. DeLorenzo, on the phone, pointed down the hall and waved goodnight. Cupping his hand over the phone, he said, "Buono Fortuna a te! [Good luck to you]." Then, Dr. DeLorenzo scurried off to see a dozen patients who always seem to flood the ER simultaneously during national and religious holidays.

Walking down the hallway wasn't the same if it was your family in an acute medical crisis. Luca shook his head back and forth. "O, my God, my God!" whispered a short, desperate prayer, "Please help!" He thought of calling the priest, but it was High Mass for Christmas. He thought the likelihood of finding a priest now was like finding the proverbial "needle in a haystack." Still, a short, squat elderly cleric walked before the physician. "Padre! Padre!" Luca called out.

The elderly priest turned around, directed his sight directly into Luca's gaze, and nodded his head up and down. "Yes, my child. How may I help?" The worried dad unloaded his anxieties before him. The priest took Luca's two hands, clasped them in his own, then interceded on behalf of the Vitalis, crossed himself, and departed. Although the physician felt better after praying, he remained alarmed and expected a lousy prognosis for both.

As a medical student and intern, he had seen the misery and painful death from placental abruption and DIC a few times. The memories of those endings gripped his attention. Most ended up in a body bag with a tag on the dead woman's big toe and left behind an empty crib, punctuating grief and pain.

Luca went to the waiting room to hear about the news concerning Anna-Claire and his son. Thumbing through the coffee table's old magazines in the lounge, he saw an English brochure about the recently discovered virus that causes acquired immunodeficiency syndrome (AIDS). Having been medically educated in Italy, he had read about patients with HIV/AIDS starting in 1982. Most initially recognized victims were gay and in the United States. The original derogatory American name was GRID (Gay-Related Immunodeficiency Disorder.)

But later evidence and cases of other victims infected with the retrovirus included IV-drug users, heterosexual mothers, children, and newborns, with a mortality rate approximating 100%! Eventually, 10,000 hemophiliacs in the United States died before Highly Active Retroviral Therapy (HAART)was available (1995), and blood banks screened all blood and blood products. He had not seen any patients associated with the disease in Italy. However, he had seen a few infants with unexplained immunodeficiency and opportunistic infections, which, according to T lymphocytes' measurement, were like severe combined immunodeficiency syndrome and had a similar pattern to their adult counterparts with AIDS.

His practice was hectic during the early days of the HIV pandemic. Initially, there was no antibody test for the virus, and AIDS was diagnosed as a syndrome (a group of disease symptoms that consistently point to the same diagnosis. In the United States, those blood transfusion patients and hemophiliacs who had received tainted blood products from patients later diagnosed with AIDS or AIDS-related complex (ARC)) came down with the same syndrome.

A sudden shock went through his heart and mind. Since the blood-transfusion relationship between AIDS and blood was becoming well-known, an uneasy foreboding fell deeply on him since Anna-Claire had received a lot of blood and blood products. These transfusions kept her from hemorrhaging to death. Could it be she received contaminated blood? Out of fatigue from the usual resident routine and drain on his body.

The dreams that followed were mystical, prophetic, and nightmarish.

Night Visions

night visions
prickly and on edge
déjà vu eerie pestilence ahead
shadows of echoes unseen
rebounding voice and step
Anna-Claire
dressed in spider's web
doused in confetti,
the pale phantom body's ebb
shadows of echoes unseen
rebounding voice and step
whirling canopies
quale banners on the coffin
colors of cherries
Scatters on the path often
shadows of echoes unseen
rebounding voice and step
candle wax and smoke
cologne kissed perfume.
smoke twirls in the dusty air
starless skies loom
shadows of echoes unseen
rebounding voice and step
empty house
our vacant bed

Anna-Claire's gone!

Anna-Claire's dead!

(Bradford Gilmore 2020)

CHAPTER FOUR:

RAGING WATERS

Dr. Alberto Maccabees, studying in Italy from Tel Aviv, shook Luca out of deep slumber. "Dr. Vitali! Dr. Vitali! Luca, wake up!" A single bright light flickered above them. Slowly opening his eyes, then startled to wakefulness, Luca sat up. It seemed so surreal all around, dreadful and beautiful mixed in disarray.

"Oh, oh! I am sorry. I must have dozed off," he replied. Rubbing his eyes awake and shaking his head, he returned to consciousness. "How is Anna-Claire? What about our son?"

Dr. Maccabees answered, "Anna-Claire has had a rough time due to the bleeding you noticed. She had an abruption and lost quite a bit of blood. Additionally, she developed DIC. We gave her six units of blood, platelets, cryoprecipitate, and fresh frozen plasma [FFP]. She is in the ICU and has stabilized. She is not on the ventilator now. Currently, she is resting. She had a C-section, but unfortunately, Dr. Vitali, we had to perform an emergency hysterectomy to save her life. But the excellent news is that your son looks healthy. His Apgar's scores were 7 and 8. He's being watched in the NICU to ensure his safety. I know it's been rough, and the next twelve hours will be critical for Anna-Claire. You are welcome to enter the ICU, but she needs to remain calm. If she wakes up, however, be brief in your conversation. I don't believe telling her about the hysterectomy would be wise until she is out of the woods, OK?"

"Yeah, sure. I won't tell Anna at this point. Thanks! Thanks for all your help, Dr. Maccabees," Luca said.

"Absolutely. You're welcome. Do you have any questions for me?" Dr. Maccabees queried.

He stated, "No…no…not right now. I am going to call to check on my other Son, Giovanni. Buon Natal Buon Natale, a te [Merry Christmas to you]. Thanks again!"

He smiled and nodded, then walked down the corridor in scrub attire, humming to some Luciano Pavarotti playing at the end of the hallway.

"Oh, God! What is their telephone number? I knew it by heart! Uh-oh, shit!" he mumbled to himself. "Oh, yeah, 051-555-1212. That's it!" he blurted out. He picked up the phone in the lobby and dialed.

"Uh, ciao, this is Anita. Who is this? Don't you know it's three-thirty in the morning?" she said groggily and sharply.

"Yes, yes. I am so sorry. I am your cousin, Luca. Luca Vitali," he replied.

"O, my God. Oh, my God, how are you? How are things with Anna-Claire? Will she be OK? How is your son? Are you still at the hospital?" Anita questioned in rapid fire.

"Yeah, yeah. I'm still at the hospital. Anna-Claire is in the intensive care unit. I haven't seen her yet, but her doctor said she is stable but had a rough go of it. He told me my son OK but in NICU to watch closely----haven't formally named him yet is in the NICU but doing well. How is Vani? I think Vani must be extremely frightened since he saw her bleeding first and came to get me," he said.

"Yes, he was, but he appears OK. You don't need to worry about him. Sincerely, Luca, don't worry about him. We are thankfully not strangers to him. Romeo and I have taken off for Christmas week through January 5, OK?" she said.

"OK…well, OK," Luca said, sighing.

"Now go see your wife and son. Take it easy; you are in all our thoughts and prayers," Anita remarked.

Luca and Anita said their good nights and hung up the phone. Wiping his brow and rubbing his temples, he first departed to see their newborn and bring some news to Anna.

The baby was laid in a warmed bassinet, breathing quickly. He could tell from the NICU hall window looking in. The charge nurse rose from the NICU desk and came to the door. Creaking open the door halfway, she whispered loudly, "Dr. Vitali! Dr. Vitali! Come here."

The Doctor walked closer. "Your son is perfect and doing fine. Do you have his name picked out?" the RN said.

"Yes, sure…umm, Orazio Antonio Vitali, but let's wait until later in the morning so I can be sure that's what we both want. Orazio means "prayer" because he is the answer to our prayers, and Antonio means "praiseworthy or priceless" because the Creator who gave him to us is worthy of much praise." Luca said. "I am pretty sure we agreed on his name."

"No problem whatsoever. How's Mom doing?" she asked.

Luca said, "I haven't seen her yet, but I know she has gone through hell. Her Doctor told me she was stable but had a rough time of it. I better see her now. Good night."

"Good night," replied the nurse. Leaving the NICU, he scuffled to the intensive care unit but stopped at the men's restroom. While in the stall, he overheard a couple of medical residents chatting at the sink. One said, "I just finished examining this young guy…oh, about twenty-six years old. He's from the States, but he looked in rough shape. He was anorexic. He also had a big tender liver, was breathing rapidly, and had pronounced lymphadenopathy. He looked jaundiced and had a fever of 390 C (102.2 F). I am still waiting on his lab work and X-rays. Do you think we should start him on antibiotics? I wonder if he's got that new American disease?"

Their voices trailed as they left the restroom. "You mean gay-related immunodeficiency (GRID)." "Yeah, it does sound like that, doesn't it?" the medical residents concluded as they left the bathroom door.

Luca furrowed his forehead and then yawned very loudly. "Hmm… probably leukemia or lymphoma with an infection or something like that," he mused." Doctors and nurses are like that…They're ready to pounce on a particular diagnosis based on the known. Still, there is more unknown and unsettled than is known. What is known or thought is often just a snapshot in the science timetable. That will plague doctors and nurses, most likely forever. Either it is discarded entirely or zigzags its way through history like Hansel and Gretel dropping tidbits as clues to its whereabouts and nature. No human being is exactly like the other. Even identical twins who share the same seed are not only biological beings. They are emotional, intellectual, and spiritual, each with unique capacities and qualities. No one, even in the same family, has the same experiences or equal temperaments or behavior. Diseases are the same way, marking their distinction from their host. What would surely kill one may not phase the other." Luca mumbled to himself.

In this manner, Dr. Vitali thought and later taught in health science classes. We may amass an exhaustive understanding of human anatomy, physiology, biochemistry, infectious and non-communicable diseases, and pathogenesis. However, the world and the surrounding universe are massive spaces where similarities and variances abound. We are all in a state of flux with our ecologies."

Anna-Claire clarified those realities to Luca in her environment, ecology, and public health studies. He loved her mind and sharp wit. He almost loved to lose debates and arguments with her to hear her version of the world, the things she advocated for and loved. To lose her to what just medically occurred would be catastrophic for him and their kids. Upon every thought of her, he thanked God and was grateful. They didn't have much in the way of possessions. That was never important or needed to them to bribe love. It flowed without hesitation and was always genuine and apparent.

As he walked toward the ICU, he tried to remember the poem he had composed during their college years. Luca was frustrated with himself for forgetting. But the man had not slept in forty-eight hours because of the medical frenzy and surreal realities he and his family were walking through. The poem was missed. No, no, it was stuck.

Dr. Vitali was always truly loved and sincerely respected by almost anyone who met him. He attracted people since childhood, like running errands for his mom in the marketplace. His personality was magnetic, and his physique, kind aquamarine, mournful eyes, and genuine smile were a joy to see and captivating. His brilliance was appreciated, and his innate sense of justice and fairness set him apart as a unique man. When he entered the ICU, he was greeted by several nurses and colleagues, who embraced him and gave him pats on the shoulder.

Finally, he went to Anna's bed; she quietly moaned and stirred beneath the covers. She had two large intravenous catheters where she received blood products and lactated Ringer's solution. Her Swan-Ganz catheter was inserted under her clavicle, showing stable values and a regular pattern, as did her ECG monitor. Her color had much improved from the time the ambulance took her. It was a great relief to Luca.

"Anna, Anna-Claire, I am here, my love. You're going to be OK. Things look like they're working out fine. Our son, Orazio, is an answer to our prayers. That is a good name for him, darling. He is alive, lively, and doing well but in the NICU for observation. That's what we want to call him, right? Darling, I love you so much," he reassured her. "Do you remember that poem I wrote you long before we married in Brescia?"

She nodded in a drowsy nod to say no because her voice was hoarse and inaudible due to the emergency intubation. Now in the ICU, she was on a face mask and receiving high-flow oxygen. The extubating following the procedure left her throat raw and tender. Luca nestled his hand over hers and squeezed gently and caressed it. He lifted it to his mouth and kissed his wife's knuckles. Then, as he massaged her feet, he remembered his poem when he decided to marry her. In a murmured tone, he recited it repeatedly:

"Do you remember now, honey?" Luca asked. She nodded affirmatively, but she winced still in pain. So, he walked over to the working crew he knew so well and asked them to give her something for her discomfort and perhaps to take the edge off. It was an awful, stark, and monstrous Christmas night.

In the corner in the dim light, there was a person, apart from the others, he recognized. He needed to remember his name. His stare got the attention of this mysterious character, and the figure rose then drew near.

"I know I have seen him before…but where? He might be the attending for the night in a crumpled white coat. When?" he muttered to himself. The man emerged from the shadows, where his features were plainer. His eyes were gray-green with an intense but captivating gaze and high cheekbones. His brown hair curled in the middle of his forehead and matched his scruffy sideburns. "Hmm, you must be Dr. Vitali…Luca, right?"

"Oh, yes. That's me. I might know you. Do I know you from somewhere?" Luca inquired.

He nodded and came closer. Suddenly, Luca knew who it was, but they had met a moment years ago. "You are Primo…Primo Rossi. Am I correct?"

Brushing back his hair with his hand, "Yes, I am, Dr. Vitali," Assistant Professor Rossi answered.

"Oh, my God! I can't believe it's you! How long has it been? It must have been eight to ten years ago. You were my Godsend during that rainy evening with my bike! How have you been? What have you been up to? Why are you up here in the ICU?" Luca questioned.

"Well, my mom and uncle got the best of me and steered me into medicine. However, I told them that if I went into med school, they would pay for a lab to explore the realm of emerging diseases. So, I had my attorney draw up the papers to finance my research, and now I have my laboratory. After three years, I got my tenure and am a spanking new "*ricercare confermato*" (a tenured assistant professor.) Primo commented. "I am genuinely interested in what has been happening in the United States and France with this new virus that destroys the host's (a person's) immune system. The French call it 'LAV, or Lymphadenopathy virus.' In the States, I think it is called the human T lymphotropic virus III [HTLV-III, the first American name for HIV). They are going to have to agree on the name. I have seen some patients with it and have sent some specimens to the Institut Pasteur in Paris. As you know, the most intriguing cases come on the weekends, evenings, and holidays. I sometimes take shifts in the ICU and Milan during the holidays to examine new patients…especially those with emerging diseases."

"Yes, I know all too well," Luca nodded and agreed. "I must attend to do some things to make my wife more comfortable. I will find you after she is resting. I'll be back in a little while. Great to see you again. What a surprise, huh?"

Dr. Rossi concurred, "Yes, it is good to see you, Luca. Please let me know if there is any way I can be of service to you and your wife while I am on call. You do need to be with your wife. She has been through a hell of a lot tonight. Maybe we can catch up when she is more comfortable and sleeping."

"OK, I would like that. See you in a bit," Dr. Vitali told him. Luca returned to Anna-Claire's bed, where she had just gotten some morphine for the pain. She was feeling more comfortable for the moment.

Again, Luca looked at her lying there. “Hi, honey. Are you feeling better now? I don’t know what I would do without you, Anna. You’ve made my life worth living, sweetheart. Thank you,” he whispered in her ear.

She nodded affirmatively. “Me, too. Yes, me too.” She spoke to her husband in a raspy and hoarse tone. Luca then nuzzled up to her and kissed her forehead with a long pause, then her cheek.

“Anna, you’re a champ. Truly, that’s what you are. I know our life has been rocky with work, the kids, and little money to get along. I am here for you. I love you so much!” Then again, he massaged her feet and calves. From the start, Luca demonstrated his affection that way, even by kissing each of Anna-Claire’s toes. With that expression of tenderness, she could rest assured that she was not alone. She was remembered. They were a team. At that point, she fell off into a deep sleep. He silhouetted in her mind as she drifted off. The world became dark. In her dreams, Luca would sometimes appear as a phantom, her husband and lover, but most of the time, her best friend and confidante. A song—a poem stirred in her sleeping mind about Luca and her bringing tranquility, something like this:

Chestnut of Skin

chestnut of skin
raven of hair
porcupine beard
organic man
chocolate bulbs
inky caterpillar bridge
Pantheon nose
Michelangelo's David
juicy vermilion smile
ivory pearls aligned
cheeks of peaches
furry cornucopia chin
neck of palm
Ural shoulder mounds
chest billows
connate man
amorous oak limbs
rapids' stones belly
mahogany buttress
luridly statuesque
tightly forked boughs
extending root pads
chipmunk-feathered toes
erect like redwoods
mysterious, sturdy

oak partner

(Brad Gilmore 2020)

CHAPTER FIVE:

THE TEMPEST

◇◇

Luca left her bed to find more coffee and a little to eat as she dozed off. It was close to 7:00 in the morning on December 26, and he headed to The Café Terzi Bologna. Anna and Luca had spent many mornings enjoying the café macchiato, pieces of bread, and pastries. It was suitable for conversation and a breakfast paradise. He recognized several of his buddies near the shop, waved hello, and walked in. The pavement was slick with the rain that had fallen during the night. The brisk and cold wind was good to awaken him more as his alertness and energy were sapped. The coffee smelled particularly rich this morning. Oh, yes, it was the day after Christmas, after all! Whew, we made it through Christmas Day with no one dying. It was not like it had been with Giuseppe.

Should he head off for the cathedral? He enjoyed Mass on Christmas Day and the days immediately following. Everyone is being taken care of in his burgeoning family. Therefore, Luca took a little time, meditated, and worshipped God. After downing his café macchiato and pastry, he hurried off to the Basilica di San Petronas to hear the chorus of sacred worship to Jesus Christ. Truthfully, he thought that all things were holding together because of the glue of his faith in God. Everything that appeared calamitous and harrowing during the night was somehow being sustained. Luca was grateful indeed. Yet, in the recesses of his mind, combined with his dream in the hospital, he was, under it all, distressed. The pipe organs struck their chords, and the choir blasted joy in every word. As awe-inspiring as the music was, his heart pined for Anna-Claire to be well. He knew her hysterectomy news would make her gloomy that no more "bambini" would come after Orazio. After the kids attend school, she could return to her career in environmental health. Still, her eyes always glistened when she played with the kids. Perhaps growing up in poverty like he had done had taught her to love people and children more than possessions or wealth. Luca thought about how grateful he was to be married to Anna. He would never forget seeing her that Christmas Eve, bleeding nearly to death, or hearing the shriek and collapsing in pain. Never!

There had been women and men who had propositioned him as a doctor for sex. But his love for her was his life, and there was no contest. Not even close! Therefore, after the Eucharist, he hurried to the hospital to check on his life's love. As he neared the hospital, he saw the ER colleague, Dr. Nick DeLorenzo, who waved him down. Jogging up to him, he said," I want to thank you for all you did to save Anna-Claire last night."

"Oh, hi, Luca. You're welcome. I have been thinking of both of you. How is she doing?" Nick asked. Nick's soft, compassionate, and sincere question was comforting and welcomed.

Luca and Nick shook hands and departed. Luca went straight to the hospital and hurried upstairs to the ICU. Anna-Claire sat up and greeted him with a smile. Her pallor still ran a colossal alarm to Luca. He kissed her ashen cheeks with tenderness. One thing caught his eye (knowing how Anna-Claire appeared before this hospitalization). He noticed her right leg to be finely curved with no swelling. However, her left leg looked edematous close to her left knee. "I will be right back," Luca assured her.

He stepped over to the ICU attending physician at the nurse's desk. He cleared his anxious throat and said, "Excuse me. I am sorry to barge into rounds, but my wife, Anna, who had the placental abruption and had DIC, has edema worsening on her left leg. She has distal redness from the popliteal area [underneath the knee]. I believe she may have a deep vein thrombosis (DVT). Could we evaluate that as soon as possible, please? Maybe something like D-dimers and ultrasound. Something like that?"

The grey-haired Doctor was considered the least amiable physician in the hospital. He was Grinch-like and snarly but often had an uncanny ability to diagnose any disease rapidly.

Moaning as he arose from his stool, he barked out, "Where is she? What's her name and yours, Doctor?"

"She is in bed 18. Her name is Anna-Claire Vitali. Mine is Luca Vitali. I am a physician in an infectious disease-immunology fellowship here."

"Oh, I have heard about you, Dr. Vitali…and your accomplishments. As you know, there are many reasons why your wife has left-sided edema and all the other complications she had on top of everything else," the aging physician said almost with sarcasm, as he was used to doing to accomplished practitioners. He slowly rose from his seat in a white coat equal to his height. It was bleached to spotless perfection, ironed, and starched. Although just a remnant of superiority from times past, the ivory layer was striking. He walked over to Anna-Claire's bed, paced in front of it, reviewed her chart's notes, left the sarcasm, and became solemn.

Luca knew something wasn't right. A considerable red alarm was flashing in his mind and made him quiver. He did his best to put on a sturdy façade, but the trembling went from his gut to his fingertips, so he hid his hands from view. It was an unusual moment. The ongoing paradigm ceased.

Pausing as if in eternity, the senior physician turned to the quaking young Doctor and looked into Luca's eyes to reach his soul. With dignity and compassion strangely mixed, this respected and often gruff elderly physician examined Anna's swollen leg,. The big bruised (ecchymosis) areas became more tender and bothersome to Anna. There was pinpoint redness (or petechiae) scattered over her arms and chest. She winced when the attending touched her knee. The elder thundered out orders. Immediately, the ICU team went to work on Anna-Claire.

Anna mumbled to Luca, "Where are the children?" Luca told her he was interrupted by the ICU staff drawing blood and performing a lower extremity ultrasound. Just as the older physician knew, she had extensive deep vein thrombosis. However, as all the staff and Luca knew, she also had DIC, and the bruising became substantial.

Pulling Luca away, the senior doctor, Dr. Paternoster, stated frankly, "Dr. Vitali, I believe your wife most likely has puerperal sepsis. Ummm, we are drawing blood cultures, CBC with diff, and platelets to be read by the pathologist. Coagulation studies and D-dimers, CPT, liver enzymes, LDH, and renal studies. We will prepare her for more blood transfusions, which she will most likely need."

Cupping his hands around the older man's ear, the venerable physician moved to a quieter corner. Luca took an anxious sigh and said in a faltering voice, "Dr. Paternoster, what should we expect to happen… umm…with my wife? Do you think she will make it?"

"Well, umm, of course, you know that is a loaded theological question, yet…I believe your wife has a good fighting chance," the elderly man stated in a wise and candid voice. "Dr. Vitali, the next twenty-four hours will give us a better idea. I suggest you take a breather now as we do our business. You must be by your wife in the coming hours and take breaks when needed. Remember, Dr. Vitali, she is your wife and not your patient. You can call me anytime or the unit if you have any questions. I will be direct with you about her condition."

"Yes, I understand," Luca said. "Thanks so much. "He walked over to Anna-Claire's bed with hesitation. The typical medical students, residents, and his friend, Primo, hurriedly got the diagnostics and treatment done quickly.

Luca's mind switched to happier moments. He remembered that day with his bike when he thought all he was doing was lost. Then Primo showed up. This teenage boy seemed all alone in the world. He pondered. Then Primo and his girl showed up and rescued him from his dilemma. Anna's husband considered the imperfect prayer the Doctor said that day. He thought he had little faith, but that was better than none. The fumbling of his rosary that day had encouraged him. Anna-Claire might pull through, and the nightmare will be over. He thought I should go to the priest where the vespers would still be going on and talk to the priest he trusted with his spiritual questions. Pulling through this crisis would indeed be a miracle. "I need a miracle," he mumbled under his breath.

Most of Luca's friends were cynical about things of faith and God. He was aware of their skepticism, yet he remembered that he thought of God as a Father as a young lad. Luca stood up for the underdogs who often had those same convictions against the schoolyard bullies, even in primary school. When he spoke with his sisters and brother about such thoughts, their criticism would burn against such tender feelings. He met with that same perspective when he attended the university. Still, it was even sharper upon going to medical school, during his training, and beyond. Now faced with the biggest crisis of his life, his young beliefs took on maturity. Would his wandering back and forth between conviction and disbelief cost him the human being he had loved the most? He remembered that he was but a mere human being full of fear and powerlessness and incapable of perfection.

Perfection? Returning to his past, he remembered wanting his dad to be flawless, but August Vitali certainly was not. The last he saw of his father was while he was in prison. Soon after, his dad's mother died on his fifteenth birthday in Luca's absence.

As a teen, he could not trust himself to be at home with himself, his mother, and his siblings. How he wished he could speak to his dad about his struggle now! Although interrupted by his father's frequent imprisonments, he had a strange affinity for Papa's strength of conviction. His father's willingness to stand up against authorities when they opposed social justice and human dignity. How proud he was that his dad, August Vitali, had deserted Benito Mussolini's troops early on during World War II! Where was he now? Absent again! Did

Luca have the strength to face life without Anna-Claire at his side? He nodded, shaking his head back and forth. How could he?

Walking over to the bed where Anna lay, there were now bags of packed red cells and platelets infusing her arms and an IV for broad-spectrum antibiotics. She was defenseless against the ravages of these unfair illnesses! Sickness and trauma are evil and our most potent enemy. Her eyes were closed, and she was sleeping. Her face was indelibly engraved in his mind. He could not take his eyes off her. Her eyelashes and eyelids showed life in the middle of her dreams. Her heart monitor showed normal rhythm but fast, and the pulmonary artery pressures were acceptable. Lifting her hand to his mouth, he kissed her fingers again with tenderness and great affection. How cold her digits felt to his warm lips! Oh, how he longed for her to wake up and the danger obliterated. Just being at home with her and the kids was his daydream. He recalled the poem he had written and sung to her when he asked her to marry him many years ago. A stirring inside him flowed with the song he hadn't thought of for years. He heard the tune dancing among pleasant memories, first silently in his head, followed by an ever-increasing crescendo into music. He didn't realize he was singing aloud or that his eyes were shut, but she moved as if harmonizing with his melody as he sang. I'm still holding a hand against his face, and his eyelids flutter awake from his sweet daydream. The room clapped in ginger applause.

Primo emerged with a tender smile out of the shadows and came forward and cradled Luca's shoulder in support. They both looked at Anna, a Raggedy Ann, indeed. They hoped for her recovery soon.

Suddenly, a thought came to mind. "What about Vani? O, my God, I don't even know!" Luca exclaimed to Primo. "I've got to see how Vani is getting along!" Doctors Vitali and Dr. Rossi approached the ICU nurse's station counter. "We will step out to see how Orazio Antonio is faring. We will be back shortly. Call us if anything changes with Anna, please. Dr. Paternoster will be up here for a while." commanded Luca.

"OK, I agree!" the charge nurse stated. "May I please have your pager numbers to call you if necessary? I am sure things will be fine." They nodded and complied.

"Thanks," they said in unison. The two doctors headed down what seemed to be an unbearably long hallway to the NICU. It seemed like they had known each other all their lives. This dichotomy was a strange affair for the physician, from the gutters to the Doctor born with a silver spoon of privilege in his mouth. Primo and Luca enjoyed a mutuality of intellect and kindness despite class and socioeconomic differences. However, the road ahead would be especially gnarly for Dr. Vitali, yet their loyalty and friendship were secure.

Primo asked, "How long have you and Anna been married? Did you guys meet in college?"

"Somewhere close to 10 years. No, we are 'high school sweethearts. "Primo, Anna has been the center and anchor of my life since age 16. You might say we live a simple life, but a happy one at that," Luca remarked pensively. "Now, with two kids. I must find a job to supplement the small stipend from my postgraduate studies. Maybe you might know where I should look. What do you think?"

"Well, you certainly have your hands full, and it will be sometime before Anna-Claire gets on her feet. I have some sway with the infectious disease department here in Milan. Maybe I can find you somewhere you could find a niche. What are you interested in doing?" Primo said confidently. "With the dean's permission, I could find a place where you could work with me if you'd want to do that."

"Wow! Really?" Luca replied. "But I might have to be with the kids and Anna more than I have. I will have to think about it, but that sounds excellent! Maybe Anna's mom and she or one of our sisters can help out. I must consider so many things now, and it's hard to think. My mind has gone in many directions in the last forty-eight hours."

"I'm sure it has, my friend," his comrade said. "I can only imagine how hard this must be for you." Luca teared up a bit at Primo's empathetic and caring words. His care for him seemed foreign, almost otherworldly. Here is the guy who helped a stranded teenager get home safely many years ago.

Luca reflected that he would have loved having an older brother like Primo. Growing up, an older brother like Primo, who had a noble character, Luca could emulate and admire. Here was a guy who understood.

They arrived at the NICU's door as both were caught up in their thoughts and conversation, after washing their hands and donning gloves and gowns to see Luca's and Anna's sons bringing a déjà vu sensation to them. Still, they moved to the inner room, where they were herded past tiny human beings to Orazio, who was already being called Tony. There he was in all his baby glory. Thank God! He was not as small as the other newborns and not on a ventilator despite being two weeks early! He had had a teeny IV going into the back of his adorable infant foot. No central lines were streaming up and down his umbilical stump, nor were any chest tubes protruding from Tony's chest. It was a relief to both physicians, as it would be with Anna-Claire.

"Anna and I have named him Orazio, but his nickname is Tony. He is so darn cute. Look. His mouth is a perfect "O" and ready to belt out a tune it looks like," Luca smiled. And softly chuckled. "He looked like he was in heaven. Just don't go there too soon! That's your Doctor's order! How is he getting along? What are his measurements so that I can tell his mom?" Luca asked.

". Would you like to hold and feed him, Dr. Vitali? It is his feeding time, "asked the neonatal intensive care unit's head nurse. "Cool. That would be great. I would love to do that," the physician said gladly. Handing Tony to Luca, he lifted him out of his warmer and stated, "Almost as soon as Luca was holding his newborn son, the intercom went off.

"Anesthesia, STAT to the adult ICU 4 in the North building! Anesthesia, STAT to the adult ICU in the North building!"

A shiver went down Luca's spine. He asked his colleague, "Do you think Anna needs anesthesia?" God, I certainly hope not!" Primo blurted out briskly. "I need to go, Luca! I must take off! I will speak to you later!" After speaking, Primo shot back to the ICU where Anna-Claire was.

Immediately, Luca began perspiring with a cold, anxious sweat. However, Tony was still feeding in his arms, and her nurse was on the other side of the NICU. What do I do? What do I do? As he paced with his little guy in his arms, the nurse caring for him saw his predicament and rushed over to help him.

"I am sure everything is just fine, Dr. Vitali. Take some slow, deep breaths. I will take him now so you can go and check on things. Godspeed, Doctor," she spoke with a reassuring tone. Orazio was securely in the nurse's arms, so he discarded his gown and bolted out the door.

A stark remembrance of his adolescent years in which his absence and his grandmama's death electrified him. His vow to never let those he knew and loved alone or to die alone raced through him—body and soul. Fear grabbed him! Strangling his breath, he scurried to see his darling, Anna-Claire. He wondered what he would find. Maybe it was not Anna at all. It might be someone else who is having trouble. He could not separate his vision of them, raising a family and a life full of her charm. If any severe complication occurred to her, his life and ballooning family would be over.

Winded from scrambling up the hallway, he reached the Adult ICU. Through the glass door, he saw a cadre of white coats clouding his view of Anna's bed. Why are they just standing there doing nothing? Then he saw his friend, Primo, at the head of her bed. The phantom of death seemed to surround the whole intensive care unit.

Consequently, no Christmas music was in the air before the two physicians strolled farther into the ICU. Frantic with fright, he moved the staff in white coats aside to view what was transpiring with his wife. Her hands were ice-cold. This was not a good sign. What had happened? His eyes were transfixed, looking at the woman of his dreams lying helplessly on the hospital cart.

"Primo…oh, Dr. Rossi, what has happened? Why did you place her on the ventilator?" he questioned urgently. "I am glad you are here, Luca. She woke up briefly and complained of severe chest pain. Her blood gases showed hypoxemia (low blood oxygen), and her breathing showed signs of fatigue. And distress. We must assume she has had a pulmonary embolism because she is too unstable to be transported down for nuclear medicine for a ventilation-perfusion (VQ scan) study or CAT scan. She has to be watched very closely. I need to ask you a few personal questions because the chart does not indicate certain preferences," he told Luca.

"Oh, my God!" Luca exclaimed. "What do you want to know?"Primo took Luca by the sleeve, pulling him to a quieter place in the corner of the unit. "I will be frank. It does not look good for Anna. Her complexity and rapidly evolving comorbidities make going forward cloudy and uncertain. I am sorry, I have to ask you. Suppose Anna should have a cardiac arrest. God forbid, what would you want for her code status?"

Again, Luca was stunned and was, in part, dissociating out of shock. He raised his voice so all the units could hear, "I want her on a full code." Then he said to Primo in a hushed tone, "I would also like to be kept current on the goings-on. Thank you so much for letting me know. Yes, I want to do all you can for her, please. I am glad you are here, buddy. Honestly, I am. Is she stable enough if I can find out what is happening with Vani at Romeo's and Anita's place?

Dr. Rossi nodded in agreement. "She is stable enough. You should call them soon. I am sure they and your relatives want to know what has transpired. Then it would be best if you took some time for yourself. Get a breath of fresh air. I am sure it will revive your spirit. I am sure Anna's going to make it. She is in good hands. Dr. Paternoster and I will give her the best care possible. As you know, the nurses here have a system of providing excellent care to the sickest of patients. Please take a break now. It still is the Christmas holiday and Incarnation Holy Week, and there was a hint of snow when I came in. See your boy and get freshened up. Take a nap. Give yourself some rest, please, Luca! OK?"

"Yes, I guess you are right. I do miss him. Vani's both adorable, smart, and sensitive. I wonder how this scene will affect him," the young pediatrician said. "OK…I will give you my cousin's telephone number." He scribbled out the numbers in a trance and told the other staff where he was going. After he waved to those working in the unit, he headed downstairs and out the side exit.

The brisk wind caught Luca by surprise. After breathing, he headed toward the parking space he always had at work. He was somewhat in a daze from all that had happened in the last two days. His mind was spinning in one direction and then the other. He reached for his tin can of a car and leaned against the door. Tears streamed down his cheeks. A nagging, draining thought plagued his mind. Will anyone be the same after this Christmas? I thought the Christmas when Giuseppe was born was the worst. Only time will tell—only time will tell.

Luca called his son, Vani, to say he had not abandoned him and reassured him of his love and care. The phone rang, and all three in the house, Romeo, Anita, and Vani, jumped and ran to the phone. This time, Vani answered the phone himself before the other two arrived. Romeo and Anita did not grab the phone away, knowing how much father and Son needed to talk. Vani answered, "Ciao," but he was too afraid to speak further.

"Ciao, Vani! It's your Papa. What have you been doing at Uncle Romeo's and Aunt Anita's house?" Papa asked.

At first, Vani did not want to talk with Papa because he was overwhelmed with fear, remorse, and sadness with some anger. " I killed

Mama and my baby brother! I cursed her, and now I killed them!!" Vani declared guiltily, feeling shame and sorrow. " Papa, when are you and Mama coming home?" the boy said, feeling his need for his parents to help him face and cope with the chaos and terror of the day. And he was afraid that Luca and Anna-Claire would never return.

CHAPTER SIX:

THE ECHOES OF THUNDER

◇◇

When the couple arrived home, it looked like Vani was sulking on the staircase. It had been where the most significant tragedy in his six-year-old life had taken place. He looked determined that it would never happen again. Her hospitalization had phased him the most. He was determined that would not be repeated. Frequently, he would block the staircase when his mom was around.

Five years post-Anna-Claire's hospitalization, everything appeared to approach normality. Vani's tenth birthday party was a delight for everyone. All Vitalis that were in the area and neighborhood friends came. Anita, Romeo, Roberto (the boys' best friend), his uncle and aunt from the farm, and Luca's and Anna-Claire's" nuclear family. Dr. Rossi and a huge surprise visit from Vani's Grandpa from jail, August Vitali! After Anna-Claire's survival in the ICU, Luca and August reconciled.

Luca visited his imprisoned dad only three times in his life. This was the last time Luca saw his father out of the penitentiary. Even Dr. Luca Vitali had sway in the justice department, and his sentence was miraculously dissolved, and the conviction was dropped. A year before his dad regained his freedom, Luca had read in the Sermon on the Mount, "So, if you are offering your gift in the Temple, and remember that your brother has something against you, leave your gift by the altar and go and make peace with your brother. Then return and offer your gift (Matthew 5:23-24 The Complete Jewish Bible CJB). Luca realized that his dad was his" brother" and that he would be his "brother's keeper" and not rest until the pardon was obtained. August's mind was changed, and even as old as he was. His many addictions ended. He no longer got drunk or in a brawl. After that, Shalom (total)peace remained in the Vitali family. When his dad joined Vani's festivity, Luca immediately got up and embraced the pardoned one. And that included his father.

But three days after the party, the night following the celebration, Anna popped a fever, and she felt she had the flu. She thought it was probably caught due to Tony's cough and snotty nose. But her armpits and neck were painful. She would wait until her physician husband returned, but Luca didn't come home until 22:08 (10:08 PM) that evening, and his wife was fast asleep. He took a brief but hot shower, which felt good to his weary body and mind. His infectious disease caseload quickly mushroomed due to the HIV/AIDS crisis. Trying to slip into bed unnoticed, Luca climbed in. Something was wrong, but what was it? The bed was warm, even hot, as he lay beside Anna. She must have come down with the flu or something like that. She was curled up, facing the opposite direction. Luca thought she needed her rest, so he let her sleep, and soon he was snoring.

Luca woke up the following morning at 6:30, like clockwork, but Anna-Claire was missing. Sleepily, he had reached over to give her a morning kiss, but she was downstairs. She was sick with something like influenza. There has been an outbreak of it on the edge of town. However, she was developing a splotchy rash he had seen on a few patients at the hospital, but it appeared nonspecific. Walking over to her and retrieving some juice, he asked, "What's wrong? You look ill."

Anna unexpectedly turned around sharply and faced her remarkable man. With a bit of anger and impatience, "Yes. I don't feel well. I have some swollen glands, a fever, and a dreadful headache. Did you bring home mononucleosis from the hospital? The kids and I already ate. Where were you that brought you home so late?" She queried emphatically.

He touched her and thought, "You're burning up.. Yes, all your glands are swollen. We should head to the ER, or you can see one of the doctors at the clinic," he reasoned. "When did you get this rash? I hadn't noticed before, honey."

"Luca, I do not want to go. I want to stay here with the children. It seems to bring an omen down on us when we go. I thought I had left the hospital for good! You already know that and do not want to go back there. I have had my fill of hospitals, and I will remain here with you and the kids. It's probably nothing anyway." she stated firmly.

"Honey, I want the best for you. However, I don't want you passing something on to the boys. I want you, my love, to rest now if I can take you to the clinic, maybe tomorrow morning. Deal?"

Anna-Claire rolled her eyes back and took a great big sigh. "Okay. You've got yourself a deal. But no more hospital stays for me. Promise me! No more. "Her rash improved in the morning, and her temperature was only mildly elevated, but her lymph nodes on both sides remained swollen. They were still enlarged in her neck, under her arms, and only slightly enlarged nodes in her groin. Beckoning Luca to come and feel them, "Things are getting better. Let's not go to the clinic. Please?"

Luca walked over and felt her lymph nodes. God forbid this being a lymphoma or leukemia or something else like it. He was starting to see acquired immune deficiency syndrome (AIDS) in his practice and at the hospital, like others had noticed in 1983. In the years following, Dr. Vitali had seen men and women who came into the hospital with diffuse lymphadenopathy and some unusual opportunistic infections. Something was dramatically wrong with their immune functioning. In those days, they called it gay-related immunodeficiency or GRID in America, but he heard women and their babies also got it. Also, he saw it in IV drug users, hemophiliacs, and infants who never had sex. No matter the source, a virus is still a virus.

Over the next week, Anna recovered her strength and was afebrile. She enjoyed caring for their kids. Her oldest, Giovanni, was a delight to her, or as she called him, "Vani." He was trying to be her helper from age five to now. He even worked harder than ever. She was the picture of encouragement and never took away a cleaning project from Vani so he'd learn how to live and work independently. Vani and his mom were incredibly close and solidly devoted to each other.

Tony always seemed to be alone, and off and on came out of his shyness and introversion. He loved to paint, which matured into the artist category in adolescence. Tony learned to play the piano, flute, and guitar, adding to his talents. The family enjoyed his music and art but gave him no credit for his schoolwork, which was average. His grades and testing needed more achievement, so he did not attend college. Like the rest of the family, he had a keen interest in biology. He excelled in anatomy but was bombed in chemistry and physics despite tutoring.

However, his struggles and other achievements were under-appreciated by his parents, especially by his father.

Everyone in the family left Tony relatively to himself, and his attachments to the family were marginalized. When he was a young boy, Tony and his friend, Roberto, played house almost every day in the first grades of school. Aria, Anna-Claire's youngest sister, and Tony would catch butterflies, moths, and other colorful insects. They loved nature but with totally different talents. Tony drew and colored these unusual organisms intricately, which was remarkable; he got an award for them once.

Although she had an athletic bent, Anna exercised less and less as time waxed on, and she got progressively thinner and thinner.

Whenever Luca would steal away from his ever-growing amount of work, he would join in on the family fun at football (soccer) games or short trips to the countryside where Anna and Luca grew up and met. The whole family loved the seashore and beaches, but this year, Anna-Claire became less interested and involved in these outings. Most of the time, Dr. Vitali, Vani, Tony, and Roberto would swim and play around the shores after her scanty involvement. As the boys matured, they (Vani, Tony, and Roberto) would play together and loved to talk and joke around. Still, the five years that separated Vani from them after he reached Tony thirteen started more and more for him to develop friendships with other adolescents his age. Also, Vani became an avid soccer player after school, and, to the point, he thought he would be a professional in high school. Although there was no rift or contention between Vani and the younger youth, Roberto and Tony, as nature would take its course, the younger boys separated from the older teen.

But as the years passed, Anna's medical problems intensified. She was resolute: "No more hospitalizations." Her lymphadenopathy had worsened; sometimes, the sheets would be drenched with her sweat, even in wintertime. At this point, Anna was willing to go to see a specialist. Afraid of making a misdiagnosis of his wife, he brought to see his colleague, Dr. Primo Rossi. Something must be wrong. It was either an infection or cancer.

"Ciao, Primo! How are you? Say, I would like you to see Anna. She has been getting night sweats almost every night and has pain in her joints and muscles, but her weight loss worries me the most. We have tried everything to have her put on some weight to no avail," Luca requested earnestly and urgently.

"Okay, I would be glad to see her and see how we can help. Bring her down to the office next to our lab in Milano next Tuesday around 14:00," Dr. Rossi said. Two weeks later, Anna and Luca headed from Bologna to Milan, about two and a half hours away. Almost the whole trip, Anna slept on Luca's shoulder. Her frail body was so bony. Her cheeks appeared hollowed out, and her eyes were becoming sunken. Her breasts, always so full in the past, were barely noticeable and flat. She was not as physically attractive as she had been. Also, the lymphadenopathy appeared more prominent. This appearance had progressed slowly over the last few months, and her weight loss had accelerated over the two weeks since the phone call with Primo.

As Anna and Luca emerged from the car, the fear of discovering cancer or AIDS diagnosis frightened them. Knowing that she had received many transfusions and blood products before, the HIV testing of blood escalated their worries. Leaning upon Luca, Anna made it up the stairs to the clinic. Winded from walking up to them, she had to sit on the bench until her husband got her. He often had to bring a wheelchair and push her into the clinic. They saw others with a similar appearance to Anna in the waiting room. Some were coughing and short of breath. Others were there with the same underlying distress. But not pulmonary.

The Vitalis made it to the nurses' station through the crowded room. "May I have your name? Which Doctor are you here to see?"

"I am Dr. Luca Vitali, and this is my wife, Anna-Claire. We are coming here to see Dr. Rossi. I am a colleague of his," Luca piped up and spoke. "We have a 14:00 appointment. Is he running behind today?"

The nurse smiled and said, "Of course…we are always running a bit behind, but I will let him know you are here, Dr. Vitali."

"Thank you," the Vitalis said together. Anna-Claire could only look at the floor while Luca paced irritatingly. Others in the waiting room got more restless, too. About forty-five minutes later, Primo arrived, entered the waiting area, and walked to the Vitalis. Professionally, Dr. Rossi greeted the two, "Ciao, Dr. Vitali, and Mrs. Vitali, it is good to see you. We will be with you while we get you a clean room, and you can come in. I have one patient before you who may need hospitalization. I will see you both soon."

Another hour passed, and then they were escorted to a fresh and spotless clinic room. "They have improved the clinic rooms and updated the patient consultation rooms, Anna. I am glad we are out of the waiting area," Luca stated with less apprehension. Anna remained silent. She appeared febrile but ashen and stared off into nowhere. Her mouth was dry, and her lips cracked. A nurse entered and obtained

Anna's vitals. Height 1.61 m (5'5") Weight 53 kg 108 pounds BMI 17.97 Temperature, 39.6 °C (103.2 °F); Pulse, 102; Respirations, 28; and Blood Pressure, 96/64.

These were worrisome, especially her rapid breathing, but not unexpected. Despite Luca's repeated insistence for her to be evaluated throughout that year, Anna steadfastly refused. Now, she was dyspneic (short of breath) and weak. She was pretty ill to herself and those who saw her in public. Her children (especially me and Tony, 15 and 11 years old, respectively) were anxious and fitful in worrying about Anna-Claire's health. You could hear Tony pray earnestly and repeatedly for his mother's health every night for the past year at home. Vani had accelerated his housekeeping to allow Anna to rest, but he also loved sports. His routine was to play athletic games after school, then rush home to prepare a quick meal, eat, do homework, and do the chores around the house. He would prod his brother to assist, which they did with reluctance.

The children were stressed about their mother's health in middle adolescence. Besides, Vani's work did not pin him to the home. He engaged in typical teenage boy antics and sexual discovery. As noted previously, Tony was a loner with fewer than a handful of close friends. He was moody, with high highs and low lows. He did have a best friend, Roberto, and they did practically everything together. Vani had moved on to older teenage friends. He was well-liked and flirtatious like many other young men; their secrets and secret lives were their own concern—- nobody else's.

Primo entered the room at the clinic, greeted the couple, and sat down with paper and pen. "Anna, when did you first notice you were ill?

I have your record from the hospital in Bologna, but I remember caring for you while you were there. Did you have any illness you remember when you returned after having Tony?"

Anna-Claire nodded. "Yes, but it felt like I had the flu. Luca wanted me to bring me here, but I have refused most medical attention until now. I don't want to be in the hospital again."

"Not one of us want that for you either, Anna. But we have to keep you well, so hospitalizations are less likely. You had that prolonged flu-like illness. How long did it last?" the Doctor asked. "Have you generally felt well over the last year or so?"

Reviewing her history and asking for more history of her present illness droned on; then, Anna fainted and was caught by Luca to avoid hitting the floor. The doctors called for nursing assistance. Anna was laid flat with her legs raised on three pillows and given nasal O2. Luca started an IV quickly, and the normal saline (NS) was infused wide-open. Primo was calling out orders.

Fortunately, the clinic and hospital were adjacent, and the orderly carted Anna to the hospital on a gurney with both doctors. The nurses drew blood, including electrolytes, kidney and liver function tests, an ELISA, and Western blot to test for HIV, T lymphocyte counts and ratio, blood cultures, troponins, flow cytometry, and arterial blood gases (ABGs). Also, the physicians ordered a chest X-ray and EKG. Primo secured a hospital bed with continuous ECG monitoring as the results were pending. She received some broad-spectrum IV antibiotics while waiting for the blood cultures and other lab tests to return, but required more oxygen.

While awaiting the HIV serology and planning a whole lymph node biopsy, Luca and Primo examined the blood work, demonstrating that her T4 lymphocytes were less than 200. The T cell subsets had an inverted ratio. The chest X-ray showed bilateral interstitial infiltrates. Her ABGs demonstrated low oxygen levels and respiratory acidosis. Kidney and liver functions were in the normal range. The blood cultures were too early to tell if Anna had bacteria or fungus in her bloodstream. Also, a hematologist and lymph node biopsies were consulted, who believed her labs were consistent with a diagnosis of an aggressive non-Hodgkin's lymphoma.

This data is what was suspected but what no one wanted for Anna. Anna-Claire had evidence of Acquired Immune Deficiency Syndrome (AIDS) plus highly aggressive AIDS-related lymphoma. The most worrisome specter was the combination of T cell counts and the infiltrates' pattern on the chest X-ray. The diagnosis of this blood cancer, both above and below the diaphragm, showed she conclusively had AIDS-related systemic lymphoma. The prognosis was dismal and truly abysmal in the 1980s. There was no treatment for both AIDS and this type of lymphoma. It wasn't until the mid-1990s that HAART (Highly Affective Antiretroviral Therapy) became available. (The life-long work of Primo and Luca was to develop a vaccine against HIV, among others.) knew of no effective antiretroviral drugs available in Italy yet. She needed a lung biopsy now, a biopsy of lung tissue to verify the suspicions of PCP Pneumocystis carini, a different organism, or some mycobacterial infection.

Luca looked at Anna and wondered if she would survive the lung biopsy. She had made it through that horrible crisis once in the ICU.

Indeed, could she make it through again? Neither of the two doctors was optimistic. Luca remembered he would never leave the side of anyone needing his care. During his absence many years ago, his grandmother's death was enough for a lifetime. Anna must not be another.

He held her hand as they prepared her for surgery. She asked, "Luca, promise me this. If it looks bad, just let me go. I do not want to remain on a ventilator longer than a week, even if I have to go on one. Promise me that, will you?" She squeezed his hand tightly.

Luca couldn't even respond to her request when she said that. Swiftly, the orderlies transported her to surgery. Anna-Claire died on a ventilator a few days following the lung biopsy. Her HIV test showed evidence, as did other blood work, that she had AIDS due to receiving blood and blood products so many years before. She also had AIDS-related lymphoma and possibly tuberculosis. The same microbial infection both of her parents died from years ago was resistant. Even if she had returned and remained long after the OR, Highly Affective Antiretroviral Therapy (HAART) was still unavailable until 1994 (5 years too late)

Primo said, "Good God!! I am so, so sorry, Luca. Anna-Claire did not make it despite life-support. I am very sorry, so sorry." Primo, who had rarely shed a tear, revealed a floodgate of tears streaking his cheeks. He then held Luca, who was limp and crushed by emotion. Primo hugged him in sympathy, but briefly. It reminded them both of when they initially met on the side of the road with a busted bike chain.

"What am I going to tell the kids—what?" he spouted in a burst of emotion while his friend said no words. Primo, who had rescued Luca on the side of the road with his bike during the violent storm in 1970, could not save Luca from the calamitous journey of life he was on now nor beyond. Dr. Rossi could and would be there for his closest friend, Luca. He could help him manage Luca's all-consuming burden, but it was impossible to take his place.

Luca called his and her relatives but had not talked yet to the children. He again called his faithful friends and family, Anita and Romeo, who immediately came to Vitali's home.

"Ciao, Romeo. This is Luca. I have some horrible news," Luca sighed and wept. "Anna is dead. Her burial site, planned years ago, will be near our old church, where Anna and I grew up, in Brescia. I don't know what to do with the kids and everything. I need to stay in Milan to tie up some things, but could you please help me assemble the funeral? "

Swallowing his emotion, Romeo said, "I will do anything for you. You know that. Anita and I will help you with the kids. Your sisters and Anna-Claire's family will, too. Aria is often around to help. We can count on her."

Primo was a comfort and Luca's number-one ally. Primo allowed his friend to grieve again. He did not say much to Luca and allowed Luca to pour his heart out. Some priests also helped in a more reserved and removed role, But Luca needed more. All his life, he bemoaned that he had no older brother or father available to talk about life's challenging issues, but Primo stuck closer than a brother. Likewise, Primo had no siblings, but his personality and welcoming spirit allowed both to enjoy brotherhood, which neither would have had without the other.

However, during the next two years following Anna-Claire's death, Luca carved out some time to think, mainly in the midnight darkness without the children.

CHAPTER SEVEN:

VICE, VENGENCE AND VANI

◇◇

My parents and Iwere very close until my mother, Anna-Claire, died. Growing up, Giovanni Vitali like my father's history of his grandmother dying on his fifteenth birthday, my mother passed away on my fifteenth birthday. Both in height and character I grew up very quickly. I was a whiz kid throughout my senior year in high school. Because of my rigorous trial in religion as a young person and I concluded that my prayers were not answered, I became disillusioned with anything that smelled like the church. I avoided it like the plague. That included any religious influence Papa and Orazio brought.

High School graduation was in the air. Robust celebrations and the chance to go out and be your own person. During high school, I was no stranger to parties, but my grades held in there, so Papa tried not to step in and allowed me a time of self-discovery. In adolescence, Papa and I lost the unity we once enjoyed. Some of the separations could be attributable to normal maturation, independence, and emancipation, but my wounds after losing Mama remained untouched and unhealed and unnoticed.

Part of it was the hatred and spite I spewed out when I saw the pregnancy causing my mother pain and sickness and, ultimately, her life, which I would recall as long as I lived. Though I was a schoolboy then, the memory of the event stuck. I was just a young boy wanting to curse whomever and whatever I could if he caused my mother discomfort. Following Tony's birth and Anna-Claire contracting HIV, I was torn between wanting to be an only child in the limelight, the "apple of my mother's eye," and my negativity toward Tony; yet I realized she gave her life to give her son "Orazio" (prayer), breath. So, Tony and I only converse sanely when another person was there. The two most common mediators of brotherly love were Papa and Roberto. As time rolled on, I left my younger brother with his friend Roberto. I found I was a magnet for sexual exploration and was sought after by several young men and women

On the other hand, Tony kept traditions and his Christian experience foremost in his mind and self-punishment over the guilt he felt being the reason Anna-Claire got into so much trouble with her health. However, there were times before I left for Oxford that Roberto, Tony, and I enjoyed when each took a break from whatever they were doing to bike in the forests, the mountains, and streams. Sometimes, we would sneak out in the night and skinny-dip together. When we were without clothes in a body of water, it seemed like ridding themselves of past baggage of guilt and loss. It was a symbolic transformation that each one felt and enjoyed, especially in their adolescence. Solidarity between the three was experienced then; and pretty much, only then.

I did defend Tony and Roberto numerous times from bullies and brutes when they opposed the younger two. Despite the deep divide between Tony and me, I would not and dare not experience the pain of losing another brother. Confusing times!

This mixture of passion, volatile emotions, and self-judgment confused Tony, Papa, and me. How to handle me as Papa's "thorn in the flesh." My father needed help with ideas. How to parent with his own personal trauma with both of his sons so young seemed impossible! Oxford might relieve the steam and was a tough school that Papa wanted for his son.

Unlike Papa and his family of origin, I did not have to be a breadwinner nor have the heavy duties of being the eldest brother to six siblings with an incarcerated dad. Although, initially, the Vitali's living was effortless, not at all lush or opulent, Papa had been saving what he could enough to send the boys wherever we wanted, like going to college in or outside of the country.

I planned on leaving to go to another country, never returning to Italy. To escape Papa, who tightly held to his Christian faith despite losing Mama. I gave up on prayer and insisted that I only go to three Masses only: Christmas, Easter, and St. Francis of Assisi Day, the patron saint of Italy. The rest, I figured, was not worth my time. Also, it was urgent to go as far as the universe would separate me from my brother, Tony, whom I blamed and cursed for all that happened to Mama, her AIDS, and her death. The tension between the two was becoming too intense and peaked because we were reminded of Mama's absence. I held resentment against Papa for not making her better which in my adolescent invincibility thought Papa had the power to do so. Nevertheless, we maintained cordiality but were distant in the same household. I wanted to extend the distance which emotions had formed. I chose the UK and Oxford University. I didn't know what subject matter interested me, but it was between social and physical sciences.

Despite the conflicts in the family, there was no loss of love or respect for each other. There was no diminution of kindness or affection but a definite need for separation and apology.

Because I was intelligent and had the aptitude for public health or medical proficiencies. I planned to attend a college in England; however, I had never been to the UK. The Bologna Agreement passed in 1999 was an initial agreement among twenty-nine countries of the European Union concerning higher education. It made education standardized and accessible to member nations. Testing and curricula were similar in EU countries, facilitating the training in a country other than your native one.

Dr. Vitali was recognized as a prominent virologist in Italy and the EU. Along with my good marks in school, I entered Oxford University. That is when our union of father and son was slowly dissolving itself.

I entered his education in England. Unfortunately, students and professors looked down on me because of my Italian roots. My black curly hair, dark Mediterranean skin, and being shorter than most British peers made me stand out like a sore thumb among his blonde and redheaded classmates. My mahogany-colored skin was a stark contrast to his pale-skinned and freckled counterparts. I searched Rosetta Stone's and Babble's linguistic training to develop a less Italian accent of his English-speaking. I imitated British television or online language sites. The Rosetta Stone helped slightly, but the TV helped the most. But although I mastered the English language in written and verbal communication, my diction didn't suit other British students. I felt the burden of discrimination, which I had never felt before.

Before attending Oxford, my academics in Italy were sterling. In England, my grades were a disappointment to my father.and myself. However, I was interested in many young women and some men because of my good looks and natural attraction.

In an essay in a preliminary course of English creative writing, I wrote: "Freedom from my father's Roman Catholicism made me realize I did not wish to be recognized as Catholic. How the Irish and the Brits fought over religion and land was abominable; these divisions were medieval. Schisms are antihuman, archaic, and better off as part of European history, not its structured future. There is injustice on both sides of that fence. Oppression and subsequent rebellion then reverse pressure until another uprising. That was a pattern throughout history. England and Ireland know it all too well. It doesn't matter if the pope is infallible; murdering someone in the name of religion was nonsense, hypocritical, and even blasphemous. The same applies to politics, blended with different faiths throughout the European and British fabric."

My grandfather was a frequent inmate because of his "aberrant political anti-Fascist" perspective, which he fought for in Italian bars in the 1930s and 1940s.. An anarchist view was more in keeping with my worldview. The structures of oppression and bigotry that damned the masses were inconsistent and needed to be opposed where they could be civil. It was best not to have an organized political system at all. Occasionally, he would spout off about it and attract young crowds, including teenagers and college students. Such speech may have adversely affected his grades.

So, I frequented London pubs to make friends and get drunk. Occasionally, the crowd became interested in me coming from the country prized as the model of romance and beauty. Often, I would find myself in a hotel room or residence with someone for a one-night stand, but rarely beyond the nocturnal heat and passion. Instead, I had no close or romantic ties whatsoever. Sex was just that, sex and nothing more. A biological experiment, that's all. I firmly believed the stunning, beautiful romance my mom and dad experienced was unique to them, extraordinary and rare. It existed nowhere else. I had never encountered a love like my Mama and Papa had personally or in viewing the relationships I saw inside my circle of friends.

Nevertheless, one friendship was stable, supportive, and fun. That person was my college roommate, Ken Morrison. Politically and religiously, we were twins. But our appearance together ruffled a lot of feathers. We were easily spotted in a crowd. Ken was tall, white-skinned with many freckles and auburn hair, but not muscular like I was. I was dark, shorter, and athletic. Often, Ken's voice was rough and crackly yet booming. my voice was smooth, seductive, and enticing. We would get louder when we went to a tavern and had a few too many. Ken was hot-headed but intelligent and a master of debate. He regularly picked fights and ended up in barroom brawls like my grandfather. Still, he was never arrested, picked up, or cuffed by a bobby for unknown reasons. Maybe it was the luck of the Irish. His mother was from Ireland, and his dad was a Scotsman. Ken taught me about Karl Marx and Friedrich Engels. It was on the same political wavelength I heard from my family, stemming back to Papa's dad. I began to appreciate why his grandpa spent so much time on the brink fighting against current conservative Italian politics and the likes of Benito Mussolini.

My grades began to slide from fatigue, stress, and alcohol. The demands of being a student made me question whether to continue or drop out. I had gone to Oxford, assuming I would get a professional degree in medicine or public health. As poorly as I was performing academically, those professions became a distant reality. Papa was embarrassed by my behavior and poor execution of my studies. So, one morning, the Doctor telephone-called me about what was happening.

"Hello, hello," the Doctor said with a moderately noticeable Italian accent. "Is there anyone there?" Due to his routine, my father woke up every day at five. Saturday was the same for him. Dr. Vitali was at the hospital by 6:15 and had a knack for being overly punctual. This morning, his schedule for the day was incredibly hectic. He had three new admissions to the wards besides the rest of his inpatients and consults to round on. He was an attending doctor, took and taught medical students on rounds discussing the latest medicine. He had the best bedside manner imaginable. However, he only rounded with the medical students and residents during the week. Therefore, this was his day, free from those responsibilities.

Eventually, a fellow dormitory classmate picked up the phone. "Hey, who is this? What do you want? It's six in the morning on Saturday, sir!" Before Luca could get a word in edgewise, the phone clicked off. Again, he called the long-distance operator to connect him. He let the phone ring and ring until someone had to pick it up. This time, it was more cordial. A red-haired youth who had gotten drunk with Vani the night before hurried down the hallway.

It was my college roommate, Ken Morrison, who just happened to be Vani's roommate. He answered in his typical Scottish accent. "Hi. May I help you, please? Hello, are you still there?"

"I would like to talk to Giovanni Vitali if he is around." Dr. Vitali quickly replied but with a huskier Italian pronunciation. Sometimes, especially when he would get angry, his eloquent air of refinement got ruffled, and he spoke with more earthy parlance like he had as an impoverished boy. "Ciao, is Giovanni Vitali around?"

Ken asked more cautiously before getting me, who had partied all night, "May I ask who is calling?" Ken knew that my dad and I were not on good terms and that I let him know the scoop about my religious dad and the fighting that had gone on before I left. Picking up on Ken speaking in hushed tones, Papa knew something was up. In such situations, my father would occasionally say he was one of my Italian friends from Tuscany, Italy, where they had lived for a short time several summers ago.Papa pretended to be a friend from there this time and mimicked his friend's speaking to a tee.

"Oh, okay. I'll get Vani. Please hold on." Ken assured the Doctor. "It will be a few minutes. Please wait. Thanks." However, I had gotten up and was in the shower. With an intense hang-over, I was trying to wake up for the day, which was difficult for me, but more so this morning. Ken saw me with soap on my face and shaking my jet-black hair. I was not ready to be disturbed, especially by a phone call from my dad.

"Hey, Vani, you've got a long-distance call from Italy…I guess from Tuscany." I soaped up immediately, washed my whole anatomy briefly, and entered the hall. However, I dried and wrapped myself in a towel in my haste while heading down the corridor.

I was still buzzed from the night before. My vision was slightly off kilter and my head was pounding. I enthusiastically picked up the phone, expecting to be talking to one of my Tuscan buddies, whom I heard was flying into England that weekend. I snorted and cleared his throat, "Ciao, questo è, Adolfo? Sono io. Vani Vitali lo sai Ciao, is this Adolfo?] Come to stai amico? (Meaning, it is me. Vani Vitali! You know. How are you, mate?")

Papa, stressed for time, answered, "Hello, Vani. Is that you? You sound a little rough. How are things going?" I bristled so much in shock and anger that my towel fell to the floor. Unaware that I was stark naked, fellow students giggled and chuckled raucously as they passed by in the corridor. One of them picked up my towel and snapped my butt cheek with it.

"Ouch," I blurted out. I immediately came to alertness. My nudity and Dr. Vitali's voice and intonation challenged me. I tried to hide the embarrassment and anxiety in my voice. "Ciao, Papa. How are you? Is something wrong? Why are you calling here? It's so early!'

Papa could not stop the flush of anger on his face but realized nurses and other doctors at work surrounded him. He took a sigh with a groan and cleared my throat as well. "Giovanni, I hear you are doing poorly in your studies. What is wrong? What is going on out there?" he questioned gruffly, as only a parent could. "I will see you next weekend and see for myself."

I knew the gig was up. Luca never called me "Giovanni" unless I was in deep trouble.

"Papa, can we talk about it later? It sounds like you're busy at work. I can see you and Tony at the end of the month. I am not going to summer school here. I could work on Uncle Romeo's dad's farm over the summer like before."

Papa let me off the hook, realizing how late it was getting and the stack of chart were s piling up. That is this time. Repositioning himself to look more professional, he said sternly but calmly, "Okay, Giovanni. I am expecting good grades in school this semester. I didn't send you to Oxford to get drunk and debauched continually like the rumors I've heard about you. Come home then; you can stay at Bruno's farm in the summer. I am sure he can use the help. I will talk with them about it. Vani, get to work, and I want to hear an excellent report when you come. Tony is graduating at the end of the month and wants to see you, and Aria misses you a lot. Son, make me proud!"

I thought, If I can't make you proud of me just like I am, you won't be pleased. I again realized the nakedness of my anatomy and recent behavior. "Ciao, Papa. See you soon," I said hurriedly. "Ciao," Papa replied. They hung up simultaneously, and the conversation closed abruptly, to their relief.

Luca wiped the sweat off his brow and said, "Well, maybe Oxford is not the right place for him. Maybe we can find the right place locally or at least in Italy where he could study better. He'll be fine." My dad thought that if Mama were here, she would know what to do. This single-parent thing is for the birds!

I was horrified that I would see my dad when I was in rough shape. This horror was especially true when I acted dishonorably, debauched, and drunk. I knew Papa would be hurt deeply unless a change took place. Despite my constant urge for alcohol, I knew I could tough it out until I took my exams and returned to Italy. There was no point in staying in England. As far as I could see, there was no future at Oxford, Cambridge, or any other British or non-Italian European university.

I was relieved I was leaving and dismayed that I'd probably lose contact with Ken, my closest buddy and confidante in the United Kingdom. I was terrified of letting Papa see me in this condition. However, perhaps living in Brescia or close to Papa's sisters, brothers, and my cousins would sober me up. I knew Papa loved him deeply, but he could not replace Anna-Claire's affection for me. I reasoned, "Papa is a kind man and compassionate. He is known for standing behind and encouraging people, making him a great physician. However, he is always swamped with work and is often easily distracted from conversations I've had with him. I don't want to disappoint him." I told Ken.

Ken replied, "Truthfully, Vani, you must return to Italy. It sounds like your dad cares but also expects a lot, right? I'll miss you, but we can keep our friendship despite the distance. I truly believe that. It would help if you had your homeland and your family. I can tell. So, let's get to work preparing for our finals. Then we can have a party we'll never forget before you go!"

Ken was one of those brilliant guys who didn't have to study hard to get good grades and was studying nuclear physics. This "brain" of the Morrison clan will go far, everyone thought, and have a glorious future.

However, that was not true of his friend. I would have to work my butt off to improve my lousy grades. This task would be challenging at Oxford with English as a second language. I buckled down to study hard. I can set goals and stick to them to very end, but needed encouragement.

Exams were in three weeks, and I wondered if I would even pull off a C on any of the courses and final exams 75% of the grade! I recalled the vision that had stayed with me since my first years in school before my mother died. I had a recurring nightmare when she was alive and ill after her death. I had to grow up fast and furiously to handle the pressure of being the firstborn. It was a bit much for a boy in his teens to take. My mom and I were extraordinarily close, but her terminal illness also strained it. I continually thought about whether things had been different and happier with her. Papa was no Anna-Claire. No one, not even Papa ,would ever take her place. That was the recurring vision of her halo and in her shadow I found comfort and solace. Her radiance seemed permanent and assured me that she would be with me wherever I might go.

After studying hard and falling asleep at my desk, a phantom like shadow came then left quickly. I had this plaguing dream recurrently draining me with a yearning to be with her and sort out the confusion in my life. "Where are you, Mama?" Like his Papa, I got glimpses of her ghost at times of stress and discouragement. I would see her with no evidence of illness in a grey-green mist and her hair blowing frolickingly. At times, for some reason, I contemplated suicide momentarily because I disappointed my departed Mama and Papa.

Despite the rough beginning in college, I quickly became well-liked, made buddies and lovers, and became popular with the university's pub-goers. Because we loved the ocean and reclining on the beach during school breaks, we looked forward to finding the sweet repose under starlit nights and full moons far from Oxford. We had numerous times when we got into mischief and paid for it, but getting into trouble was often our forté. We had one last desire to go to the ocean shores before departing on uncertain terms and my return to Italy's intrigues.

We could find an ideal place to "get laid," Ken thought openly, and for kicks, get into another brawl together against the Neo-Nazis in that area outside the metropolis. Both of us young lads hated right-wing groups that populated the seaside location we were headed. Maybe these genes of anti- "fascism/anti-Nazism" ran deep in my blood. The genetic component fits my grandfather's temperament toward the Mussolini regime in WWII. Papa's father, August Vitali, was hunted down often for his pro-socialist views and imprisoned throughout Papa's childhood and adolescence. My dad would tell the stories of his escapades, occasionally with admiration and a sense of pride but mostly with scorn and ridicule. This weekend being my last with my best friend meant that this had to be the time to do both simultaneously. Let's go!

Enthusiastically, we headed to the shore, feeling our oats and sowing our seed. It was a perfect day to swim, get inebriated, and find the right gal to sleep with. Tuesday, the day following our last final exam, was perfect for swimming and swimming at the end of May. We had our sandwiches of pickled pork and mutton sandwich with sides of mayo and horseradish, which had only suited the Italian palate that day. I could stomach it once more. Then that's it! Unfortunately, little did I know it would be my last supper with Ken Morrison.

As I had always done for occasions like this, I had my camera and notepad handy. Sometimes, the adventures were so elevated as to write a journal note or a poem about them.

At the shore, we stripped down to our trunks. I always looked tan, especially compared to my red-haired mate. Ken was as white as birch bark, freckled, and could burn quickly under the hot sun, but I seemingly could absorb the sun through pane glass windows.

Today would be a fateful "ocean day" for Ken and me. After our day in the sun and excursion to the most infamous bordello, I jotted down this poem and called it "Anemic in the Rivers of Blood." We headed out to the tavern of ill repute at the end of our day. We were ready to find the perfect or at least available women of the night.

Maggie Sue's was a well-known brothel and bar where sensual pleasures were developed to their zenith. However, the tavern was a sizeable ramshackle edifice, having multiple enchanting bedrooms. Some of the rooms had mirrors below on the floor and up on the ceiling and covered the thin walls. Others had satin sheets and one pillow. Each had its loo. Maggie even remembered contraception and condoms.

As expected, the front door was painted crimson on a door with several layers of paint and golden doorknobs. Above it, Maggie Sue displayed a neon sign reading Maggie Sue's Pub of Entertainment and Delights---Open 24 hours and Low-Cost Rooms available," Vacancy."

The front door was jammed stuck, frustrating Ken and me so we pounded on the door for entrance. Maggie Sue herself greeted the boys. "Hey, boys!" she said in her seductive Mae West imitation. "Is that a banana in your pocket, or are you happy to see me? Ha-ha--good old Mae West! She knew how to talk with men! Good to have you here. We have lots of beer and booze, and drink until you drop! We have many hot women, or for that matter, a few young men to show you a good time if you're that kind of guy. Appetizers are free after you drink four mugs of beer or have two cocktails. On Tuesdays, the bedrooms are free to new customers. Since I haven't seen you before, you're the new birds of the evening! Go ahead. There is plenty of entertainment,"

Maggie Sue was initially from Plano, Texas. Still, she inherited the pub from Hermann Bradley's uncle about twenty years before the young men entered. The owner was attractive but dressed in burgundy vintage hooker clothes from the early part of the twentieth century. She was medium height, a buxom, fair-skinned, wavy brunette wearing long hair down to her waist. She wore tons of make-up plastering her face, lavender eye shadow with fake long eyelashes. She seemed to be in her late forties or early fifties. Other women circling were in their late teens and twenties.

The bar was a sight to behold. Although the building's exterior needed lots of work and repair, the interior was crazy but classy and immaculate. Bottles of every kind of spirit you could dream of and kegs of beer, but they only had a few bottles of wine. I quickly found a young woman, Sadie, and disappeared into a room to mess around.

"Get me a pitcher and four shots of Jack Daniel's," Ken demanded and pounded the bar. They brought it to him promptly with a plate of appetizers. The more Ken drank loosened his tongue and attracted many patrons, including a gang of Neo-Nazis.

Anemic in Rivers of Red

Embers clothed us both at eventide.
with smoke imperceivably.
Coals still radiating lava at dawn.
My hair was short and burnished black
His, the color of strawberries in the wild
with lily-white skin be-speckled in cloves.
I whispered exuberantly,
"Red, the crimson waves
arrive, breaking through to greet us."
Yes, Red and I swam.
out in aquamarine waters.
But the stop sign never squelched our fun.
We played and splashed.
alongside the ivory cliffs and coast,
dotting it with realgar ash
We stalked on the cliffs of Majolica Earth to see crystal streams.
of paradise's engorged bosom.
pausing, we turned toward town.
The jaunt felt timeless.
as we abled arm' n arm.
setting out for Maggie Rose's tavern.
Imbibing his usual sangria drenched in burgundy,
Red stood the bar aloft, speaking hoarsely,
debating wildly while reciting
Marxist lingo in toto.

Raging, burning with anger and passion,
my friend, with flaming irreverence,
buttonholed the first skinhead seen,
though an Aryan giant was twice his size.
A quick-tempered flush upon their cheeks
flashed downward, engulfing.
engorged neck, ruddy torso, and iron belly
sweep with Adonis's ichor and veins bulging.
punch each other senseless, reaping bright gore.
soaking tables, chairs, and floor.
The rest gather steam cannibalistically fashion,
yet my Red stands tall while being.
pummeled, raises the "sickle and hammer!
The Nazis stack up their wounded.
bloodied as tomatoes against the brick wall.
Red grabs me, pulling me through the whore's door.
Holding his gushing gash,
we make it inside the empty barn.
As I lay him on a bed of hay,
a foreboding pallor descends
masking his rubied flamboyance.
Weakly, he pleads my name.
The butchery is now apparent.
seeps from wounds like a sieve.
All anger and politics dismissed,
Claret spots envelop his thinly veiled carcass.
Salmon ribbons of flesh punctuate the scene.

In anguish, I sobbed over and over again.
Then I grow ashen during a brumal sweat.
frostbiting my skin and ligaments, muscles, and bones.
I shake, staring at my bloodless buddy: eyes fixed,
wounds too late for clotting,
the necrosing aroma of death.
white turning blue.
anemic in rivers of red.

(from *Wisdom for the Weeping Widow* by Bradford Gilmore (AgapePhileoEros 2021)

That was a fateful day for them both. Ken was gutted with one of the fascist blades in the tavern. I didn't know what to do in the scene. I got my friend out and away from the tavern's pandemonium. With all my strength, I dragged Ken, limping as I began the incline. I knew of a nearby farmer's house up the hill; maybe an ambulance could make it here in time; perhaps one could be heaven-sent, but it was at least a dozen miles away from the nearest hospital, and whether that hospital would have appropriate life support and blood to help resuscitate, Ken was a mystery. If only we had chosen a better town nearby like they had mentioned, but Maggie Sue's allures changed our direction. "Can I leave him here like this?" I repeatedly asked myself I trekked up the hill. I was covered in Ken's blood from holding my companion as the day dawned. I appeared scarlet, red as sin, in Ken's blood upon opening the door to the farmer's wife.

She screamed, "Oh, my God. Oh, my God! Harry, call the police! Call the police right now!" She took the broom for the porch and pointed it like a rifle. I was nearly convulsing with pain, dread and fear. My hair was splattered with blood, and my breath smelled dank with liquor. My jeans and shirt were lacerated. My left calf was slashed, and blood quickly poured into my shoes.

Harry came running out from the back bedroom with tattered, half-unzipped jeans and a wine-stained white T-shirt that partially covered his distended belly. "I called the police, but it will take a bit for them to get out here, and I let a doctor know that the ambulance would take an extended time to arrive. Here are some towels. Put pressure on it, Millie!" He barked out.

I felt faint and was ashen. My head was swimming while my pulse was thread-like and fast. Suddenly, I vomited my pickled pork, mutton sandwich, and a belly full of booze. I collapsed on the steps to the farmhouse's backdoor with my light-headedness. The couple roused me and laid Ken beside me in the barn until the authorities arrived. Ken was immobile but still breathing and bleeding like a sieve when they put him beside me in the barn. Ken died 30 minutes later. When he expired, I held my buddy in a fog; all warmth left his corpse.

Racing through my mind, I fearfully repeatedly asked the existential question. "Why is there so much blood? Inescapable! Blood everywhere! Not a drop within my veins!"

Although I had been at the beach and crimson blood-drenched them, my clothes were of high quality and Italian fabric. My tan face proclaimed my Italian heritage without having said a word. The police arrived first just as Ken breathed his last breath; an ambulance came 20 minutes later. I began to go to in a mixed, semi-lucid state, attempting to answer their questions, but I spoke to them in my foreign tongue. The ambulance and police officers got me to the nearest hospital and called the surgeon on duty to care for my wounds and stitch me up. But I had hemorrhaged and was severely anemic. Even though the hospital was small, they had several units of packed red blood cells of my blood type and gave me two units, and then my color and sensorium partially returned.

The older Doctor asked, “Who are you, son? Where are you from?”

“I am Giovanni Vitali. I attend Oxford school, but I am originally from Bologna, Italy,” I replied. The name rang a bell with the physician. He asked, “Are you Dr. Vitali’s relative?”

“Yes, I am…hmmm…I am his son,” the young man said. “I am Dr. Luca Vitali’s son.”

Looking into my eyes, the elderly physician said, “Do you know how to reach him?”

Before he spoke a word, my vision momentarily flashed red, and everything around me vanished from sight into a scarlet blur. I was in deep trouble and needed Papa’s help. , But I was also reluctant to let him know about everything. Yes, I was petrified about what would and could possibly happen to me in a foreign country. It appeared to the uninformed that I was guilty of the murder of my best friend, Ken, whom I loved heart and soul, without sexual intimacy. I questioned how this would break my father’s heart to seem in peril and disgrace. Whether Papa would believe my innocence. “I am not sure. He works day and night in many hospitals with Dr. Rossi and Professor Primo Rossi. I don’t have those numbers. They are back at the school, Oxford

University. Still, if you call the University of Bologna, you might be able to find him through Professor Primo Rossi. What should I do?" I inquired.

The senior physician hesitated. It seemed like he paused forever. Rubbing his wrinkled chin, it was apparent this was a puzzle to him. "Sir, I will call the university to retrieve your father's information. May I have your permission to do so?" the Doctor queried. Stung with anxiety at the possibility of them calling Oxford, tremulousness and diaphoresis soaked my face and body. Even as distant as I was from Papa on religious and moral issues, I was confident that my father would know what to do. Maybe call a lawyer or the Italian Embassy or something of that nature. My brain was filled with the flashes of Maggie Sue's before and after the mayhem that followed. I not only realized that my best friend was now dead but that I would be one of the prime suspects in his murder.

That night haunted me and would dog me for the rest of my life. I had no alibi. But I also had no motive. I was one of the ones responsible for the brawl, but it took place at a place locals called a "whorehouse," which Maggie Sue's tavern was famous for in the local area. Also, that night, I had spent in the arms of a "woman of the night." How would that look in court, at the embassy, and with my father? Indeed,my student visa would soon be null and void. Facing a court in a foreign country was one thing, but confronting the mess I got into with my dad and family was an entirely different ball of wax. "Yes, you can contact them," I stuttered shamefully. The physician nodded in agreement and then talked with the police officer.

My clothes were covered in blood and smelled of vomit and liquor. The policeman came into the room, put me in cuffs, and stood to block the door until the physician returned. Dr. Jenkins, the older man, returned. I started to mourn for Ken, and then I lamented the guilt and shame of that night.

"Well, we got a hold of the registrar's office and obtained your father's phone numbers, but we couldn't reach him. I must let the police officers know you are well enough to take you to the police station. They need you to answer some questions, you know?" I nodded in discouragement. What would more happen to me there? I did not know. I felt guilt, shame, and sorrow for that fateful night. Indeed, they would have also contacted the Morrisons, Ken's parents, who were lovely people but already broken by the drowning death of Ken's closest niece.

I got my mug shot and fingerprints on record at the station, strip-searched, and changed into prisoner's clothes. Two officers booked and escorted me to the holding cell, holding three additional prisoners. All of them were taller than I was. The three were muscle-bound, although one had a big belly due to his overdrinking. They were some from the gang of Neo-Nazis that Ken, and I encountered at Maggie Sue's the night before. This situation was not going too well. No, not at all.

All three had no visible hair on their head with black stubbly beards. One of them, David Waterhouse, was covered with tattoos, mainly serpents, demonic sayings, and Asian lettering around his waist. Despite his body's markings, he was the only one with good looks. His arms were thickly muscled and covered with black hair. He had an angry look on his face that never changed. He had two chipped and pointed teeth, which were razor-sharp. His features were fierce but weirdly attractive. His neck was as thick as a tree trunk. His eyes were bloodshot and blue, but he had cuts and bruising above his right eye from the night before.

The next surly character was named Johnny Oats. He was about six and a half feet tall. His face was oval, and he had shifty hazel eyes. One black eyebrow covered both eyes. His nose was broken and engorged on both lips, which bore multiple cuts. He was the most buff and sinewy. He had been in many brawls, which were intentional and under his plan to disrupt. Numerous scars covered his face and trunk. Some were self-inflicted cigarette burns. He had one continuous tattoo. It was the image of one strand of green barbwire with its prongs dripping blood.

The shortest of the three was still taller than I am. Mark Wiesenberger was the one with the protuberant belly. His skin displayed a yellow-brown hue, and he spoked with a dry smoker's voice. His teeth were ghastly green, and the whites of his eye lightly yellow. His arms were as bald as his head and covered with bruises at all stages of development. His ears were flush with his head and covered with silver and black studs. His tattoos were indistinct and tended to run over each other. Each of them had a green swastika tattoo behind their right ear.

The three showed wounds from the fight between us the night before. The scowling and mocking started softly but rapidly piqued in a crescendo. Their intimidation was cruel and sadistic. This night was not as good as the last had been before Ken died. Horror crept on my face, and my usual strength dissipated utterly. I peed my pants and dripped on the floor before skinheads, inaudibly saying, "Here I am…rape me!" The three sized me up, and one right after the other spit at me, encircling me, licked their lips as if they were a pack of wolves ready to pounce like they had hurt someone similarly before. They started a chant relaying with each of the three contributing.

"Payback time. Not so strong without your mate, Mr. Burnt Pizza, are you!" Johnny, the trio leader, said with a snarly grin of the devil, "You too made such a lovely couple…yeah, a couple of homos. Faggots! I hate faggots! You know what we do with them, foreign faggots! Time to give you a ride, you, Mr. Guido stallion."

David mockingly said, "Each of us will eat you like a meatball, and when you're bleeding, we'll slurp you up like a bowl of spaghetti! Hey, guys, let's take our turn and eat the pasta. Who thought he was Mr. Strongman last night!" The tension and apprehension blanched my body in a cold sweat. Cornered, I banged on the door to no avail. I was caught in a vice with no way out. I shrieked so that someone might hear what was going on, but no one came to my rescue. But Mark and Johnny ripped my clothes off me, and then all three banged me repeatedly as they threatened me.

When the seven officers reached the door, I lay on the floor in a pool of red and brown bloody excrement, a broken nose, and new bruises. The attack seriously injured me. Limp, I was hauled out of the cell and rushed that night to the hospital for the second time in ripped and bloody garments and partially covered by a hospital blanket.

Immediately, I was admitted, rushed to the operating room, and evaluated for more critical internal bleeding. Fortunately, it did not occur this time, although I had lost a lot of blood. To be sexually assaulted as a man was both physically damaging and psychosocially damning and has life-long sequelae. However, the social degradation violated the "macho" image of myself rattled around in my mind. That was no longer possible. Being "macho" was a game and mask of my own vulnerability.

Association with Ken's slaying was horrifying, and absolute dread was inevitable. I figured I would be reprehensible to my dad, family, and friends on multiple accounts. I was so sure of rejection by everyone. I did not realize that later, Would I ever be a hero ever again?

Dazed and confused, I woke up bandaged and receiving blood and antibiotics again. Another Dr. Jenkins was at my side writing notes as he reviewed the chart. "Looks like you have had your fill of brawls, my friend." He walked over and shook my hand. "You are Dr. Vitali's son, right?"

At first, my grip was weak and impotent, but as the Doctor withdrew his hand, I grabbed it like a vice, saying, "Don't leave me. I am frightened out of my mind. I won't survive another fight---please don't send me back to the jail cell; I'll die there!" But I was usually more detached and unemotional, and certainly never in a panic, but I was like everyone else in what I'd experienced this time.

I'd gotten through in a daze, and my future looked dark post-operatively. Now, I sobbed uncontrollably. To be raped repeatedly by three men lingered and would repeat itself in episodes of post-traumatic stress disorder throughout my life. "Papa won't understand. No, he won't get it at all., Papa was furious about my grades, but being raped and arrested for murder would crush him. I am so ashamed. I've dishonored him. Will I ruin Dad's medical practice, which he has worked hard to build? It echoed in my mind. I knew no one else could remedy the situation. But I was convinced Papa would be wounded but never defeated.

Again, I contemplated suicide and meditated on how I would end my life. As vexed as I felt, I could not do that for my father's sake. Papa was a single dad with two kids and was overworked infectious disease specialist who never had much time to meditate or grieve his immense losses of Anna-Claire and Giuseppe. He still carried guilt about leaving his grandma on his fifteenth birthday. Yet, he always seemed to praise and encourage us and others in our troubles, no matter how old we were. No self-harm and death. Not this time!

Shamefaced, I looked up and pled for mercy from the treating physician. "Please, please, can you help me? Please, please!" The physician looked at me, knowing I would not survive another fight.

"We're here to help you, friend," the younger Dr. Jenkins softly stated, patting my hand reassuringly. "We have gotten a hold of your father. His plane should be here by now. I am sure he'll be here shortly!" At that moment, I could see my father rapidly approaching where I lay. Papa's pace went ever faster as he saw me in the hospital room before him. My father talked with doctors, asking questions down the long hallway. He was still in his scrubs from Milan! It looked to me and those around him that Dr. Vitali took no time to change before grabbing the flight from Milan to London.

Out of breath and sweaty, Papa reached my cot. He took one look at me, and simultaneously, he threw his arms around my neck and kissed me on his cheek and forehead. "I knew something wasn't right when I heard you on the phone, Vani. I have been so worried about you. We'll work this out. Don't worry. We will!" Papa said confidently, and both of us wept and reconciled with each other.

"Papa, I am so sorry. I'm so sorry. I..." I could not say another word and wailed uncontrollably.

"It will take some time to recover, but when you're stable, we will bring you back home…where you belong. I have called my lawyer and the embassy. We'll get this worked out." The movement intensified the pain, and Papa called my nurse, who gave me a hefty dose of morphine. Then I fell fast asleep on my father's shoulder.

Another loss of the magnitude Luca had with Anna's demise would be his end. I could have died: he had to be at my side and make the flight to London as quickly as possible. There was no time to get prettied up. After Papa's grandmother's death on his fifteenth birthday, the engraved response was a constant reminder to be at the side of anyone in peril and with his children without hesitation, without question.

Things were on the mend between Papa and me. When I came home to Bologna. It took time for me to recover and sort out all the legal matters. I could not have done without my dad. Papa got lawyer, the embassy, and some help from Oxford. He knew what to do in civil and legal matters and since he was proficient in English, Italian, German and Hungarian, Papa could negotiate and arbitrate as an advocate for me.The trial in the UK was severe but was just and even-handed despite my foreign origin. For the conviction of murder, I was fully exonerated, and the charge was expunged from my record; however, I had to pay Ken's and my part 10,000 Euros for the damage to Maggie Sue's property during the brawl we had with the swastika tattooed fascists. Papa was so kind and settled most of the fees, and then Maggie Sue dropped the charges. However, Papa wanted me to continue being sober and stay out of fights. I met with the Italian Alcoholics Anonymous groups in Bologna every day for 90 days, got a sponsor, and talked to papa often.

On the other hand, Mark, David, and Johnny, who raped, tortured, attempted murder, and violated me, were sentenced to 50 years in prison for their crimes! Fortunately, the three were imprisoned not only for their crimes toward me, but had weapons charges for the stockpile of semi-automatic rifles and hand guns they collected to sell to fascist buyers, They were part of a far right wing clandestine group smuggling firearms. A conviction of their hate toward communists and foreign-born immigrants or on visas was considered; the length of their incarcerations was augmented because they had done the same to three other men. All of them were hate crimes against *young, assumed' gay* men of college age. Fortunately, a witness gave point-by-point details of the fight and came forward soon after the murder.

The summer was nearly half over, so I recovered enough to do some chores at the farm I loved. I worked there for several summers before going back to college. Tony, was home but didn't know what to ask about my injuries and trouble with the law. That would come in time.

CHAPTER EIGHT:

THE VULNERABLE AND VANI'S VICTORY: HEROISM FROM THE HEART

◇◇

Tall Tony's porcelain face
Hair with eyebrows dark as ebony
And emerald eyes of a doe.
Smile Complete sets white as seagulls free.

Gone away, bluebird.
Gone today.

Roberto's curly raven locks
The frame of a paragon teen
Raphael Canvas's deep chestnut eyes
Ruddy brushstrokes keen

Gone away, bluebird.
Gone today.

Fused hearts are torn apart.
Boyhood dreams were gay.
Brass and gold alloyed.

Sensual passions allay.
Gone away, bluebird.
Gone to stay.
---Bradford Gilmore, 2020

Tony's most remarkable features were his intense, woeful-looking, doe-shaped emerald-green eyes, long eyelashes, and full ebony brow, appearing more mature than his actual age. His thick, curly hair needed a barber's cut to bring out its wave. His cheeks were high, with a full Grecian nose arched between each. His full lips, winning smile, and porcelain white teeth characterized a genuine tenderness unique to Tony. His face yielded natural blushes upon exercise, excitement, or embarrassment. He was taller than me but less muscular. He was thin but not gaunt. However, his calves and thighs were those of a speedy runner. Possibly, this was due to him sprinting away from bullies who chased him. He could run a long way and do well, for instance, in the three marathons he ran over the last two years and was well-known in Brescia and even as far as Milan for his speed. Tony praised Giovanni, who was surprising and courageous because he often stood up for him and Roberto. When they were in middle school and high school at the same time, Giovanni was Tony's hero.

Roberto had moved north from outside Rome with raven black hair and chestnut-colored eyes, which always twinkled on top of a dark-skinned face. A thin, brush-painted adolescent beard encircled a broad, dazzling grin punctuated by symmetric dimples.

Both young men initially came from scarce means and shared acolytes' duties at the Basilica of St. Mary Magdalene. Roberto and

Tony were attentive to prayer at the parish cathedral. They religiously and frequently went for confession and absolution. Both had visions of being priests, but life has a way of snatching dreams away.

Tony was less brilliant and received poorer grades than I. Tony was more artistic than he was scholarly. Roberto had an encyclopedic knowledge of biology, chemistry, and physics; I excelled in math and did brilliant work in physical and social sciences. Roberto and I enjoyed helping with Tony's schooling. All of us would go for walks or movies together. We joked and teased each other often. However, before graduating from high school, I had a rekindling and nurturing of spite for Tony---in my mind, I kept blaming him for Anna-Claire's death. Tony's birth was the product of an injurious pregnancy and delivery requiring massive transfusions that were inadvertently contaminated with HIV. In some ways, before going to college, I blamed Papa for not being able to cure her like he was supposed to. But much more profound, I blamed myself for not being able to rescue her because he was at home and the first to see Mama when she started bleeding. Also, I blamed and cursed Christmas Day and the Church for fractured nativity for killing my mom. Although the thoughts were irrational, I held onto them as accurate, I had to blame someone or something. With free floating accusations, I held everyone responsible and no counseling could dislodge them. Tony's and Papa's faith was illogical and harmful. I would alleviate my inner turmoil by getting away from both of them.

From buddy play to buddy hug to buddy love to human desire, Roberto and Tony started a progression to self-discovery, sexual identity, and bonding affection. At age seventeen, they calendared the day they would disclose their intimate bond to their parents but Roberto and Tony were scared as hell!

Tony told Papa and me before Roberto did. He spruced up, shaved, styled his hair, and dressed in a suit and tie. He lightly put on his father's Versace cologne. For some reason, this helped Tony relax and feel valued and in control. Then, he headed downstairs to the kitchen and found me and Papa washing dishes and drinking coffee together. The kitchen table was cleared of all plates and food; the only remaining was a small vase with four freshly picked butterfly flowers. Tony found it odd and wonderful at the same time. Four flowers mystically showed him that Papa, himself, Roberto, and I were separate individuals yet unified. The flowers' petals were yellow, red, purple, and blue. The multicolored flowers, like the gay flag and the number of blooms, represent acceptance. Was this a good or bad omen?

"Papa and Vani, I have something to tell you. It might make you angry, even hate me. But I need to let you know something about me. It means a lot to me, so please hear me out. Before speaking, let me finish. You know Roberto and I have been friends since birth. Well, you see...you see, hmmm. He and I have been in love ever since Vani left for Oxford. I don't know what more to say about it. It is a fact, and the love we have is special. We ask for your support, not necessarily to believe anything differently than you do now. We want your acceptance not because you agree with us but because you love us." Tony said, trembling. When Tony told his dad, Luca left the table without saying a word. It confused Tony about what that action meant, but he did not pursue an answer. He kept it to himself.

With kind, accepting eyes, I said, "Tony, you know I love you, and for that matter, Roberto, also. I always saw you two as very close even though we all enjoyed each other's company and "brotherhood." I never thought you were gay nor wanted that type of love and affection. However, I am irritated that you couldn't trust me enough to tell me before now. I accept you and Roberto, but I don't understand your beliefs. Tell me if I'm wrong, but do you and will you stay with The Church that strongly teaches against it? I never thought you well-churched boys would come to that decision or conclusion about yourselves. I support and love you no matter what, but I don't see eye to eye with you. Papa is upset or disillusioned by you telling us this news. He may be hurt by what you said. In such circumstances, he may believe he raised you wrong or if Mama was here, it would be different. He felt the same about me because of what happened in England. Maybe Papa feels sad, guilty, or ashamed about you like he thought about me. I am sure he did not know what to say or how to react. That's why Papa got up and left. He's a good man and always comes through for all his kids. I know he loves you through it all. Grant him some time to sort things out. He needs time to think about it for himself."

Relieved by the softness and unexpected tenderness of the moment, tears ran down Tony's face. He exited the table and embraced me for a few minutes. "Thanks, Vani. You've always been there for me---thanks for being strong enough to support me despite our differences. You don't know. I am just glad you're my brother and you're home. Thank God you're alive and at home. I was worried I would never see you again because of your injuries. I'm sure Roberto would want to speak to you as well---we both want us all to be close friends.'

"Yeah, I want that, too," I replied. The brothers left as friends closer than when Anna-Claire was alive.x

Tony called Roberto right away to tell him the good news. However, Roberto's speaker was loud on his phone, and his father heard the news. Enraged, he swore he would strangle them both.

An emotional crescendo followed them down the street after Roberto said what his friend said was accurate. An emotional volcanic response made Roberto run from his parents about his homosexuality. The news of Tony and his love for each other was too distressing to his parents. An argumentative altercation between Roberto and his father ensued. Fearing for his and Tony's lives, Roberto fled from the mounting temper and physical threats his dad was making. Staying in his parent's house was not an option.

He ran to our home but met Dr. Vitali first before Tony. Immediately, Papa got a "restraining order" for child protection and was allowed to shelter Roberto at the Vitalis' for a month until the children's security dealt with the problem. During that time, Roberto's bond with Tony grew more intimate, emotional, and sexual.

After a month and the restraining order was lifted, Mr. Nicotera, Roberto's father, got a revolver and headed to the Vitali's home to murder Roberto, Tony, and anyone else who would stand in his way. I was unusually at home that day, as were Tony and Roberto. My brother's decision and orientation was his own business: neither mine nor my choice for him, but that is none of my business However, my protection and support of him was my business!.. Intriguingly, as time passed, I could handle and disperse any bullies but my own. I was now twenty-two, fit, swift, and brawny. I am not very tall, and shorter than Tony.

I worked as a farmhand for three years, and it was evident. I am all chiseled muscle and quick. I was made for such a time as this!

I could hear Mr. Nicotera shouting, "I will kill that little sucker! Little faggot! He's going to hell when I get him right between the eyes!" Mr. Nicotera was a large man of 250 lbs (114 kg). and worked in the mill in the next town. He was a short-tempered man of violence and not of reason. However, Roberto's father was a man in his late fifties, a heavy smoker and drinker. At that time, I had already stopped smoking over three years ago when I started running. People knew me, and Tony had run in several marathons for our athletic prowess and endurance. We were among the top ten runners in the Lago Maggiore Marathon and the Chianti Classico Marathon.

Three doors down from the Vitalis's residence, a neighbor heard Roberto's father shout as he approached the Vitalis's home, called the police, and told them to bring an ambulance because it would be bloody.

I snuck out the backdoor and ran into the back of the assailant. Mr. Nicotera had not noticed me behind him. I jumped from behind and miraculously wrestled him to the ground, knocking the pistol far into the street. Somehow, winning in tavern brawls paid off. I maneuvered my way to get him in a "half-Nelson" without choking himand pinned him to the ground. Roberto and Tony ran out of the house, as did the neighbors to help. During the struggle, Mr. Nicotera had a sudden cardiac arrest. I immediately noticed him go limp and quickly let him go like a hot potato. Roberto's father lay in the street, and he turned an ashen, slate-gray color with cyanotic lips. He died from tangling with me!

"Call an ambulance right away!" I yelled to his next-door neighbor. In an adrenaline explosion, I flipped Nicotera over and began CPR. "See if Romeo or Dad can help!!" Papa, Romeo, and I knew advanced CPR. Luca remembered he had an epinephrine injection and sent Roberto to fetch it.

Romeo had heard the commotion and came running from down the street in time to help me and the others in their attempt to resuscitate Mr. Nicotera. He had no response to CPR, even a solid chest thump and as a last-ditch effort of a shot of adrenaline into his heart. The injection to Roberto's dad's heart produced no response. Roberto's dad was dead. Roberto began sobbing, saying, "I killed my dad! I killed him!" Tony hugged him close with his arm around his shoulders.

Roberto's mother was coming home from work and driving down the street where her husband's body rested motionless. She slammed the brakes and flew out of her car, yelling, "Carlo! Carlo! What's wrong? Tesoro! Tesoro! Get up!" When he heard his mom cry, Roberto stopped sobbing and hurried over to hold her. Before his cardiac arrest, Mr. and Mrs. Nicoterra had a treacherous, violent relationship, the complete antithesis of Anna-Claire's and Luca's relationship. Roberto's mom often thought of killing the dead man herself after she got beaten or he abused the children.

In parallel with his father, like Luca, Tony gave up his pursuit of sexual allures after the crisis with Mr. Nicoterra--mirroring what Luca did when his grandmother died on his watch. The alloyed couple of Tony and Roberto was no more. His mother, brother, and he packed up and moved out of town to live with her extended family in Naples. Roberto's mom remarried an older Etruscan man within a year, mainly for financial reasons. Still, the marriage was violent, the Nicotera family continued to endure the same battering as before.

Roberto was literally thrown out the door of his family's home. He was back on the road, looking for a way to get his life back together. Roberto could not find another male or female lover to fill the void. Tony and he were no longer the dreamy-eyed teenage lovers they had been. They went through many tough times together, from Tony's mom to Roberto's dad's death.

Interestingly, an eight-year-old child with a candle stood at his door quietly singing the sad, lonely song in the cold blasts of December that he sang with Luca when he left Romeo and Anita's to see Anna-Claire. Mystically, the eight-year-old lad identified with Roberto's mourning and sang a song from *Les Misérables* Death to dreams, the death of hope and the death of some of the tenderness he brought to Tony's life wasted and scattered.

Like Luca, twenty or so years before, the child only said, "Remember!" The cathedral gonged loudly in Naples, making Roberto jump and take his eyes off the child. Again, almost identical to Luca's history, this mysterious child was nowhere to be found. Roberto wanted to question him about the meaning of "Remember." After a long search, he could not find the youngster. After searching every street, backstreet, and alley over the next few hours. "Remember." Remember what, who, or when?

Tony was crushed to the very core when Roberto left. There were no more intimate or shared "aha! moments". Just grief. Just pain. He went to mass and confession as many as the days would allow but found no satisfaction and felt no absolution. However, Christmastime saw other people having fun and being happy, but he was not. Following high Christmas Mass, he pulled Father Joseph aside and asked what he should do. He confessed. He had taken in the Eucharist but only found discouragement time after time. He prayed morning, noon, and night while fasting three days every week. Like some early Church Father, he stripped naked and flogged himself with a belt, but the guilt and shame only intensified.

His midnight calls to Father Joseph were repetitious and frequent. He was seriously contemplating suicide despite the heavy Catholic theology opposing its sanction. Although his Papa had grown somewhat distant, he could trust one thing: his father's humility made him feel as though he was welcome and talking to a friend, even as a confidante. Following a particularly exasperating phone call with Father Joseph, Tony climbed the stairs and, in panic, knocked on Luca's door. Initially, it was hushed. He expected his father to be fast asleep after a long day at the clinic, but he was not. To his surprise, he saw him kneeling and weeping at the side of the bed. Walking softly over to his Papa, he had never seen him like this. Raising his head to look at his son, Tony queried, "What's wrong, Papa? Why are you crying at the side of your bed? Tell me, please! What can I do to help?"

Turning, Luca gazed into Tony's emerald eyes and said, "No, son. How may I help you? I know you feel shame and guilt over what happened years ago, which makes me sad. You have tortured yourself for saying you're gay to me. Roberto was a lifeline for you, and you loved him. If love can be measured, you loved him no less than I loved your mother. I adored everything about her. She was my treasure". Tears streamed down his face like waterfalls— beautiful and life-changing. "But I turned a deaf ear and walked away and have never returned to comfort you in your grief or console you with my acceptance. I am so, so sorry, my dear son. The Lord's Spirit opened my eyes to your pain and suicidal thoughts tonight. I am here for you. Truly, I am!" When he spoke those words, all the fear, self-hatred, and grief began to melt away from Tony. "Your mother and I called you Orazio (meaning "prayer") for a reason because you are the answer to our prayers. You are, you still are!"

Immediately, Tony sank to his feet, embraced his Papa, and loudly wailed. They held each other close while choking back the rivers of tears flooding their eyes to the brim. The tension between the two of them deflated. The relief of believing and accepting yourself many times is more arduous than coming out publically.

"Tony, you probably know this psalm well already, but let me recite it."

It is Psalm 139.

Lord, you have searched me,

and you know me.

You know my sitting down and my rising.

You perceive my thoughts from afar.

You search out my path and my lying down,

and are acquainted with all my ways.

For there is no word on my tongue, behold, Yahweh, you know it altogether.

You hem me in behind and before.

You laid your hand on me.

This knowledge is beyond me.

It's lofty.

I can't attain it.

Where could I go from your spirit?

Or where could I flee from your presence?

If I ascend into heaven, you are there.

If I make my bed in Sheol, behold, you are there!

If I take the wings of the dawn,

and settle in the uttermost parts of the sea,

even there, your hand will lead me,

and your right hand will hold me.

If I say, "Surely the darkness will overwhelm me.

The light around me will be night,"

even the darkness doesn't hide from you; the night shines as the day.

The darkness is like light to you.

For you formed my inmost being.
You knit me together in my mother's womb.
I will thank you,
for I am fearfully and wonderfully made.
Your works are wonderful.
My soul knows that very well.
My frame wasn't hidden from you
when I was made in secret,
woven together in the depths of the earth.
Your eyes saw my body.
In your book, they were all written,
the days that were ordained for me,
when there were none of them.
How precious to me are your thoughts, God!
How vast is their sum!
If I count them, they are more in number than the sand.
When I wake up, I am still with you…
Search me, God, and know my heart.
Try me and know my thoughts.
See if there is any wicked way in me,
and lead me in an everlasting way.
—Psalm 139 (World English Bible)

"Tony, God knows all about us, even the hidden things in our lives," Luca continued. "Whether you are old or young, He is the one who knows about all our deepest fears, your inconsolable yearnings and the things sometimes we call darkness. His presence illuminates it all. When we let Him lead us, there is a peace we can palpate. His understanding is outside the religious paradigms we would safely construct for ourselves. That is why having the Spirit teaching us is critical for our faith and trust in God."

Scooting to Tony, Luca put his arm over Tony's shoulder, kissed his forehead gently, and reassured him that a father's love doesn't disappear or suddenly evaporate. Then they stood up and headed toward the kitchen for a cup of coffee, even though it was three in the morning.

As he walked with Tony, he said, "Sometimes we make God too small. Tony, you are genuine. I like and love you the way you are. I like that you are not someone else. Please know that well and be confident in it.. You are kind, gentle, and warm like a young St. Francis of Assisi. One thing I know for sure: I won't give up loving you, okay? Never!"

Sniffling, Tony replied, "Okay, Papa,"

"You are my son. No one can take that away from you. Maybe that's the same with Jesus. Please let me know anytime you are bullied or feel suicidal. The sooner we deal with it, the better. Suicide is not the answer to loss," Luca continued. "When we lost your mom, I thought my life would and must end myself. But then I grabbed hold of myself and said, 'You have children who need you. You have friends and the rest of the family who need you. And for me, I must take care of others, too. Maybe you and Roberto will meet again. Perhaps that's what will happen, Tony, or become like St. Francis of Assisi."

"I sure hope so, but until then, my nights are dark, and the sun won't rise. Nothing but perpetual clouds reign over our love," responded the young man. Papa said, "Nights can be so long when you lose the love of your life."

Meanwhile, I had my day in court. Fortunately for me, one of the patrons at Maggie Sue's and the woman of the night I had slept with that fateful night came forward with evidence and alibis proclaiming my innocence. She was carrying my child, which a paternity test had confirmed. After discovering I would be a father, I went to England and brought her and the baby back to Italy: the young woman, Sadie Robbins, and their baby's name, Alessandro. Sadie was happy but afraid about living in Italy and having a son. I continued working at Bruno's farm and enjoyed taking over the reins when Romeo's dad could no longer manage the farm.

Roberto Nicotera stayed briefly with his family after moving outside Florence, where his mom moved. After the man his mom had been sleeping with took charge of the family, it was time to leave. Roberto was thrown out of the house like a piece of garbage. His orientation was rarely discussed positively. Although brilliant and intellectual, he was also physically attractive and had a pleasant and kind demeanor.

Sadly, urban and rural communities had no place for him to dwell or work. Roberto first started begging, but no one wanted to see a beggar. Sometimes, he'd sleep on the cathedral's stairs until a cop would come along and push him down the street. Several times, gangs of young men beat him up. One time severe enough to knock him unconscious. A "charity hospital" took him in, only to send him out as soon as he awoke. But most of the time, he slept on any couch in any condition at his drug dealer's place or had to sell his body for bread and drugs to dull the pain.

Survival sex, they call it. When the only sustenance you have is by prostituting yourself for a few euros, enough for bread, you do it and hope things will improve. Only drugs can remove an empty belly's pain from being used like a ragdoll. It is the circular path of satisfaction and despair, from life to death, repeated a million times. At times, Roberto would stare into the puddles at his mirrored reflection after the rain fell, with only the minutest hope of getting out of this life and having a new beginning.

CHAPTER NINE:

PREDICTIONS, THEORIES, AND OTHER REALITIES

Aria's lifestyle was simple, down-to-earth, and academic. As Papa had done in his life, she wanted to pursue a career in studying and teaching about public health and climate change. She had been able to fly back and forth to Australia growing up because Luca was a prominent virologist and was well-known worldwide. He frequently was invited to lecture on proposed HIV vaccine development and immunovirology. During these trips, Dr. Primo Rossi would accompany Luca and his sister-in-law. Both doctors were often invited together due to their conjoined work in novel therapies, diagnostics, and vaccines. Primo's lab continued to expand. Both spent half their time in academics, writing scholarly articles for the medical and scientific communities, and half treating and diagnosing patients.

When they would take these excursions to Australia, the three would rest, spending as much time as possible either in the wild or viewing the Great Coral Reef. Invariably, this would ignite conversations around climate change and biodiversity loss. They saw considerable heat increase and prolonged heat waves with drier weather each time they went.

In December 2002, the Chinese government invited Primo and Luca to evaluate a coronavirus epidemic starting in Foshan, Guangdong, China. The disease characteristics were fever, shortness of breath, dry cough, and influenza-like illness. However, it often developed into a severe acute respiratory syndrome (SARS), a picture consistent with acute respiratory distress syndrome (ARDS), which they had seen as the aftermath of sepsis, shock, pancreatitis, fat emboli, and others. (Anna-Claire experienced ARDS many years ago after Tony's birth and her abruptio placentae. Aria wanted to join the doctors to go and evaluate what was happening from an environmental standpoint. She was intently fascinated by how climate change affected the microbial environment and the increasing frequency and global spread of pandemics. However, the Chinese government refused to let anyone except these two virologists help stem the epidemic of coronavirus infection, SARS-CoV-1. Initially, the source was suspected to be a zoonosis, but the animal from which it spread remained elusive. It took two years to bring the outbreak under control, and it had spread internationally to twenty-nine countries with a 16.4 percent case fatality rate.

Additionally, the HIV pandemic reached every continent and claimed more than 40 million lives. Therefore, Primo's and Luca's keen interest lies in developing a vaccine against HIV. Despite HAART, the infection killed about a million individuals per year. Part of the tragedy, like with Vitali's, is that children are orphaned by one or both parents. This was a vast catastrophe hitting developing countries, especially in Africa. Worldwide, most of the new cases of AIDS were in heterosexual individuals, which was different in the West.

Next to the window, Aria was looking out of the plane, seeing the great seas and ocean, and saw denuded areas where forests that used to be lush and green were overrun by human activity and filled with large urban areas. The earth's defilement and deforestation showed human flagrant disregard for nature and forest fires, especially hitting Australia and North America hard.

Aria proposed a theory to her brother-in-law and Dr. Rossi in the jet. "Luca, I hypothesize that there is a direct relationship between biodiversity loss and viral pandemics. You have told me that these coronaviruses may be found in many different species. But what if rapid population expansion, deforestation, or dry riverbanks were the leading causes of global infectious disease outbursts in a region formerly unexplored or tampered with by humanity, leading to ground swell unexposed to one of these unknown viruses? That sounds like the makings of a more extensive viral pandemic. I predict this will not happen once, either, Papa! As we destroy nature, she will destroy us. It won't just be in or because of China either!" Aria stressed.

"Well, yes, that is possible in theory. Good idea. That is an excellent idea. We will keep that in mind as we search for a source. You're on to something there, Aria! You are so smart. Your sister would be as proud of you as I am! I think you should do your dissertation on something of this nature," Luca stated.

Primo piped in, "We have the genetic sequence. Luca, let's get back to the lab and start working on a vaccine before this gets out of hand." Primo, Aria, and Luca left immediately.

The Chinese government attempted to hide the SARS-CoV-1 epidemic. From November 2002 until April 2003, China kept the world and the World Health Organization in the dark until the virus spilled over her borders. In Italy, Luca and Primo set to work. They had been some of the privileged few to know about the science behind the virus. As they expected, the virus causing the first SARS was a coronavirus common to a bat population. But how did the coronavirus jump species from bats to humans and then human-to-human transfer? Can an effective vaccine be made where coronaviruses can't skirt host defenses? Would it be more like a murine (mouse) or feline (cat) coronavirus? Would the vaccine also be effective and produce durable/long-lived immunity or cause an immune response that killed the cat? These are the questions Primo and Luca set out to find answers to as they attempted to develop vaccines.

A group of virologists made the vaccines and produced highly neutralizing antibody titers. Yet they led to a pulmonary hypersensitivity reaction (in lab animals to the vaccine and exposure to the SARS-CoV-1 virus, which did not occur in controls in experimental models.

"What is causing this hypersensitivity reaction?" Luca questioned Primo. "How can we modify the immune response but still maintain the potency? Do we need to reduce the "chemokine" (immune-related components like interleukin (IL) and tumor necrosis factor (TNF) storm that appears to be occurring in some patients?"

Primo rubbed his chin and demonstrated a puzzled look, wrinkling up his forehead brows. "Luca, I think you may be right…maybe? Blocking the interleukin production might be helpful to immune-modulate, maybe? What is the mechanism for some to be asymptomatic and others to have a fatal outcome? A lot of head-scratching to come, I guess!"

Both Doctor Rossi, Doctor Vitali, and Aria came to "an understanding that although viruses are the smallest of beings, they can do horrendous damage so extensive it could stop the human race in its wake." Luca and Primo stated in teaching at various medical schools nationwide, "Literally, the smallest, unseen microbe can turn the world and its systems upside down. Smallpox and H1N1 influenza are excellent examples of how microorganisms can stop national and worldwide commerce and destroy global swaths of humanity. Without antiretroviral therapy against HIV, the disease without an effective vaccine would be nearly uniformly fatal, and the pandemic would have slaughtered millions more people than it already has. One million or more people die yearly from HIV/AIDS and related diseases. Despite being so tiny, it can bring death, catastrophe, and disability to every infected individual. Smallpox and measles before vaccinations slaughtered an immense swath of the unimmunized public with no collective immunity. Before there were any microbiologists, it was known that particular diseases, that is, infectious diseases, have distinct patterns of who gets sick and who doesn't. Whether planned or not, most Native Americans did not have immunity to the organisms European colonists brought to the Americas; large sections of their tribes died as a result. Intermixing of the European people groups with Native Americans often yielded disastrous results of microbial genocide. The closer the proximity of people, the quicker infections became plagues and certain deaths. That has remained the same for millennia since the dawn of time. Where there is not a large enough herd immunity (communities of those immune to the infection), groups of unvaccinated or those resistant through contagion, the likelihood of how swiftly these viruses spread from person to person is apparent."

These three scientists (Aria, Dr. Rossi, and Dr. Vitali) and a couple of public health geniuses, Anthony Fauci and Michael Osterholm, warned others that there would be massive, earth-shattering, and life-destroying viral epidemics after they saw the speedy spread of SARS-1 in 2002 and Ebola virus crisis in 2014-2016. With the extensive global pandemics, they believe that containment of the virus through such simple means as condoms, wearing a mask, handwashing, uniformly disposing of, and social distancing would at least slow the viral spread. It was just common sense! During the so-called "Black Death,"" the Great Pestilence," known as the bubonic Plague in Europe in the 1300s, killed off one-third to one-half of the European population. Although, it turned out not to be a virus, Yersinia pestis, but a bacteria carried by infected fleas on the backs of rodents. Once sanitation was in place, this plague abated. Simple procedures can be done in lieu of, before, and after effective vaccinations become available. Unfortunately, our pride, stubbornness, convenience-based culture, and ignorance of medical history play an enormous role today. Handwashing, hygiene, and social distancing continue to mitigate against further viral spread. It is easy stuff to do when you do not understand a disease or infection. Seven centuries ago, this became evident with no science to justify it. In this technological era and snobbery of our day, boasting our intellect and scientific knowledge, we snub uncomplicated methods to solve complicated problems."

Also, Primo and Luca, sometimes with Aria, frequently attempted to make a vaccine to prevent or treat HIV. In addition to their frustration over HIV infection, their attempts to produce a long-lived effective vaccine yielded only ineffective antibodies. It was not protective. Likewise, after over 40 years, there remains no viable vaccine to replace the current use of antiviral medications; HAART, condoms, and circumcision remain the most effective public health measures against acquiring HIV. The same has been confirmed with several vaccines against HIV. Even though antibody production may be high, protection did not work with drug companies on many antiretroviral therapies; however, as most physicians know and can predict, there will be a day when antiretroviral medications fail, and the virus becomes resistant. HIV continues to mutate rapidly. The key to all infectious disease control is prevention, not treatment.

As Ben Franklin said, "An ounce of prevention is worth a pound of cure" (1736); it is better to prevent something from happening than treat it when it does. The phrase "a stitch in time saves nine" by Thomas Fuller (1732) means addressing things quickly and more efficiently is better than waiting and putting much more effort, time, and money into ending something. This attitude was the ethic that both physicians agreed upon. Understanding each disease and its pathogenesis early could lead to knowing how to contain it quickly and give clues on how to prevent illness by a vaccine, which was their life's work and passion.

CHAPTER TEN:

PHYSICIAN HEAL THYSELF

After the children left an empty nest at home, Papa moved to Milan to continue his work with Primo and eventually acquired a professorship in one of the medical schools. The stress of being without his Anna-Claire and the labor demands continually took their toll on Luca.

He ran up the stairs to his lab that January 2018 morning to be punctual as usual for a small conference. Primo and the other doctors had just started discussing their plans for an urgent mission to the African continent due to the rapid spread of the Ebola virus in Central and Western Africa.

Luca sat in the back of the conference room, trying to catch his breath. His face wrinkled in pain, and he started breathing heavily and rapidly. He squealed out as best he could, "Someone, help me! Hurry!" A cold sweat from top to bottom clung to him like syrup, and he could not catch his breath as if a tiger had bitten his neck and left shoulder. His agony was excruciating and did not abate with rest only. Grabbing his shoulder, he panted out, "Primo! Primo!"

Luca had gotten Primo's attention first due to his ashen appearance, loud breathing, and struggling for air. Primo led the meeting. "Luca," Primo howled," what's wrong?" Although Primo was more advanced in years, he leaped off the podium and ran to his friend. Others immediately rose from their seats, eyeing Luca's misery; immediately, Primo knew. He alerted the other doctors in the room. Most of the room's medical professionals were well acquainted with men and women with heart attacks or cardiac arrest and knew the signs and symptoms down to a tee. Suddenly, the room was abuzz with activity. If the doctor stopped breathing, medical students ran to get an Ambu bag and oxygen canister from an often unused storage closet. A nurse brought wet washcloths to wipe off the sweat calmly and prepared Luca for transport to the Emergency Room and get an ECG.

A young female cardiologist who would join the team got to Luca second to get to Dr. Vitali's side, pulled out her stethoscope as a nurse ran, and unwittingly got a blood pressure cuff the team had brought to the meeting. The woman physician read out "162/91." His pulse is 110. The group breathed a little easier. Dr. Vitali's blood pressure and heart rate were elevated due to the physician's pain, and he did not have hypotension (low blood pressure), which would indicate an impending arrest.

"Amyl nitrite is, in my bag, there is a tiny dark brown bottle of nitro...or Nitrostat.. in it. Get it and bring it to me right now!" the doctor ordered the senior female medical student. She immediately knew what the bottle looked like but told the doctor. Luca snorted a small amount of nitrite since no one could find the tiny Nitrostat pill to put under his tongue. Immediately, another in the group finally brought it to her. "Now place this under your tongue, Dr. Vitali," she encouraged.

Luca began feeling the nitro taking effect with a fuzzy feeling under his and a pounding headache. The pain in his chest, shoulder, and neck began subsiding, and he was starting to breathe easier.

"Have you ever had this in the past? I mean, have you ever had this type of pain before? And the shortness of breath new?" the cardiologist queried.

"Just a few times before, but not this severe. I have had either one," Luca replied. "I don't know anyone having heart disease in my family… no. I always carry some Nitrostat and a small vial of amyl nitrate in case someone else has heart trouble. I guess that someone would be me! As they say, 'Physician, heal thyself.' Oh yeah, maybe my paternal grandfather died young from cardiac arrest."

"We would like to take you to the hospital, run some tests, and get an ECG on you," the cardiologist said.

" Oh…okay…I guess yeah, sure thing," Luca agreed. An ambulance was called. Primo accompanied him, and he was immediately shuttled into the emergency department. Tests revealed an elevated troponin level, and ECG showed evidence that Luca had had a mild heart attack. He was taken to the cardiac catheterization lab. The circumflex coronary artery was 95 percent occluded, and the diagonal artery was 85 percent blocked. Dr. Barone placed one coronary artery stent in each of the blocked vessels. His recovery was uneventful. His color was back to normal, and there was far less pain.

Primo was in the hospital room when Luca returned." How's my favorite doctor?" Luca questioned Primo with a reassuring grin as he woke up after heavy sedation in a solo, dimly lit hospital room.

Primo replied, "Me? I was going to ask you the same question. Ha-ha! I am fine, but today's event shook me up with you." Primo gave him a stern look like a father would do. You know I am the team's senior member, moving into my golden years, and now you have had myocardial infarction [MI]. You are not the one who is supposed to get sick here. I don't know what to do now. We planned to visit Sierra Leone and the Democratic Republic of the Congo (DRC) next month. I told you about the Ebola virus outbreak in Western and Central Africa. The first cases were noted last December, and we planned to be there on February 13 or 15. We have personal protective equipment [PPE], nurses, doctors, lab techs, and a solo medical resident, Ugo Sabatini, ready for the trip. Ugo's a whiz kid. He is a quick and good-natured lad who will be doing a fellowship in infectious diseases and immunology starting in the summer. Maybe he'll be the next Dr. Luca Vitali! Ha! Ha! Maybe be another!" Primo uttered.

"No. I say Primo Rossi if he's lucky!" Luca chimed in. Primo came over to his friend for decades with a wink and a smile. He came over to the bedside and said, "No! There is only one Luca Vitali, who I picked up on the side of the road. No, there is no one like you!"

"No, you can't get rid of me that fast!" Luca said with a chuckle. "I'll be running circles around you both in no time. When you told me about Africa's epidemic, it piqued my interest. Maybe we Europeans, Italians, can give back what our fathers stole from Africa. I know that Tony thought of going to a mission site in Africa. Ah. Shoot, I can't remember where it was!"

Dr.Rossi said, "Well, Luca, we need you to set up the lab. You are not going with us; there is no chance of that happening. So, get that out of your head! It would be best if you had cardiopulmonary rehabilitation so we can continue working on the Ebola vaccine. You need the rest. Let's see how things go. Maybe we'll go together next time."

"Are you bringing that kind of cardiologist with you? Is she part of the team going?" Dr. Vitali inquired.

"Yes, Luca, she is, and I haven't told you or anyone that she has accepted my proposal to be married after we return from Africa. We plan to leave in six weeks, and you will still be on the mend for the next few months. Please keep this to yourself until we get back!" Primo demanded.

"Vani is at home and has taken up from where he left off. He's been through hell and back and has young Alessandro to raise himself, yet he is always willing to help me when I need him. Also, Vani got me to buy life and disability insurance and sign a will!"

"You could find an accountant or even a public health director. The public health guys know about the finances to run a medical project. I have one in mind I have worked with before and would choose him---he's ethical and reliable. However, his name and number I don't recall; I think they are on my desk."

Luca was still lying as flat as a board with a compression dressing and a sort of vice applying pressure to his groin over the femoral artery through which they had done the coronary artery procedures. He stated, "But, but… OK. You're right, of course. You're right. Congratulations on your and the cardiac doctor's engagement. I knew if you had to wait until age sixty-five to find the perfect woman, bully for you! Way to go, pal! I hope you are happy you waited. I am sorry I didn't ask; what is her name again?"

Dr. Rossi replied, "Oh, yeah. I am sorry you haven't met until today, but you will like her. She's a gem. Her name is Isabella-Margot. Yep, Isabella-Margot Barone," Primo said proudly. "She is from Rome, but she went to Harvard Medical School in the United States and did her Internal Medicine training at George Washington University, then went to the Cleveland Clinic to study cardiology. We met at a seminar at New York University, and the romance began. At George Washington, she was encouraged to consider global health since it's engraved in her to reach middle- to low-income countries like Sierra Leone.

"Primo, it looks like you're robbing the cradle! She can't be over forty years old, right?" said Dr. Vitali. Dr. Rossi back, his locks straightened up, and said, "Pretty good guess, Luca, pretty good guess! I guess we have fallen in love with the baby in the crib! She's thirty-eight years old and sharp as a tack! Plus, she's pure dynamite to feast your eyes on. By the way, I have talked with her, and you're welcome to stay with us. There is no need to move, but we will want you on the ground level, and we'll take the upstairs. Does that arrangement work for you?"

"Well, yes. Are you sure? That is very generous of you. Are you sure?" Dr. Vitali replied.

"Yes, of course. I know you will like the female physician. She's fun and humorous, smart yet very amiable and compassionate. She must be like what you have described Anna-Claire to be. Luca, you should date again, I think. I think you should. I do!" Primo stated frankly.

"Let's not talk about that again. I have memories of Anna and my children. That is enough for me," Dr. Vitali said slightly annoyedly. Just then, a lovely Persian nurse walked in.

Coming around to the left side of the bed, she released the clamp that had been on him for at least a few hours. Her name was Bakhita Tehrani Ibrahim, and she had just been accepted to medical school at Columbia University in the States. Brimming with contentment and reveling in her accomplishment, she said, "Hello, doctors. I wanted to be the one to care for you, Dr. Vitali, and tell you both that I just was accepted to medical school at Columbia University. Have you ever been to the United States or New York City? I thought you might have gone there in your travels," she said gleefully. "I have come to take the vice grip off and ask if you needed something for discomfort or to eat or drink."

"That's excellent news! Congratulations!" they both said together. "What an achievement! "Thanks a lot, Primo. Dr. Rossi and I have visited New York City several times, and he and I toured Columbia University and New York University a few years back. We have attended American and International Conferences on HIV/AIDS several times. "

"Well, I should be going. Isabella is waiting for me. Good night, Luca, and goodnight, Miss Future Physician!" Dr. Rossi said and patted Luca on the shoulder and waved goodbye as he walked out of the room, then came back and said, "I did call Vani and Orazio, I mean Tony, and they said they wanted to be close and see you. They should be in town in the evening. Orazio should be here about midday tomorrow. I will try in the morning. Good night again!"

Nurse Ibrahim smiled and nodded. "He sure is a nice guy and a great doctor to all his patients. Can I bring anything you need right now, Dr. Vitali?" "Yes. Something for the headache and lying flat for hours. Yes, and a little something to drink and eat would be nice," Luca answered, nodding affirmatively. "By the way, when do you start your medical studies? Please keep us updated on your progress, future Dr. Ibrahim!"

"I will leave to go to the United States at the end of the summer. And yeah, thanks. I will keep you in the loop. I will get the medications and something to eat and drink. I'll be back shortly," Bakhita said with a big smile.

Luca received his pain and cardiac medications and a little snack and fell asleep. Also, Nurse Bakhita brought an ice pack for his headache and asked if he would enjoy music since the Easter holiday was around the corner.

Luca responded quickly, "O yes, please. Possibly, I can hear Handel's Messiah. I went to the London Philharmonic's rendition a few Christmases ago. I'd appreciate it---it brings me some comfort because I always remember that Christmas when Anna-Claire nearly died after delivering Tony. I want to let that memory go, but it still is a tie with my wife. She was the world to me. An angel without duplication! Both at Easter and Christmas times, I listen to the Messiah."

"I am sure you loved her a lot, and I know you did all you could to prevent her death stated Bakhita. She found a recording of Handel's magnificent work, and Luca found it lovely that a Muslim woman would find his most precious treasure. "I will locate Handel's Messiah so you can hear and see the singers and the orchestra. One time, I heard it, and believe it or not, it almost converted me from being a Muslim into a Christian, but that would break my parents' hearts. I couldn't imagine doing that. However, Handel's Messiah gave me a new appreciation of the Christian faith. We believe in Isus, in Arabic or Jesus (Hebrew

Yeshua) in many of the same aspects, and Handel's Messiah brings out those beliefs."

In the morning, Luca looked around to see who had been at his bedside when he saw Orazio (Tony) looking out the window and praying softly. He wore a brown cloak with a hood and a white rope around his waist. Bare feet in the winter cold and at thirty-three years old, had been a Franciscan lay brother for four years and sought holy orders in Assisi regardless of his gay sexuality. Since the parting of Roberto and him, he had remained entirely celibate and lived near St. Francis of Assisi's town.

"Tony, come over here, please! So good to see you! Thanks so much for coming so quickly. I hope to be going home tomorrow or later tonight. How are you, son?" Papa asked.

"I am doing well. Thank you. How are you feeling, Papa? Are you better than yesterday? Dr. Rossi got a hold of me at the abbey. What happened, and what did they find?" Tony pleaded.

Luca could finally sit up independently without having the restriction of lying flat. "Well, it wasn't too much, but it looks like I had a little heart attack. I am not worried about it, but I haven't seen any doctors this morning. How are you, Tony? What's new in Tony's world?"

"I will tell you in time. I want you to get some good nutrition for you to heal faster. It looks like the staff is bringing your breakfast in to eat. I am worried about you, Papa. You're sick so young and are working yourself into an early grave. Have you started smoking again?" Orazio answered.

"No, I haven't been smoking lately. I smoked that short time after your Mama died, but none in years," Luca replied. "How is it in the abbey, Tony? What are you doing there?"

"Well, Papa, because of Mama's illness and death and having friends who died from AIDS, I have started some groups to educate the poor, the IV drug users, and the gay community about preventing oneself from getting HIV. And to tell our family's story. I traveled for the abbey to Rome, Florence, and even Bologna, not far away from where we used to live," Tony said thoughtfully.

Luca smiled in appreciation, saying, "I am very proud of you, son, and I know Mama is too. I meant to ask you for some time. Do you ever hear from Roberto Nicotera? Have you been in contact with him? I am curious and concerned to know if he is doing well."

"When Roberto left, as you know, I was devastated. I thought that it would be the last time I would see him. I saw him when I was several miles outside the abbey. I was praying and walking north, and he was walking south on the other side of the road. I looked up and saw him, and I knew it was Roberto. I don't think he recognized me, at least not initially. I didn't know how to get a hold of him. But suddenly, after many years, we were on each other's path. I couldn't believe it! I said, 'Roberto, Roberto Nicotera. How are you?' Hello, my dear friend'". I spoke. "He looked dumbfounded and not very well. We turned back toward the abbey. He grabbed my sleeve and asked, 'Is that you, Tony Vitali?'

‹Yes, it is. It›s me, Tony!› I replied. «Suddenly, the tears welled in our eyes, and we just held each other, crying. ‹I can›t believe it!› we both said repeatedly. It had been years, many years, Papa.»

"I am sure you were overjoyed to see each other. But you said that Roberto was not well. What's wrong, Tony, if I may ask?" Dr. Vitali asked, fixing his eyes on Tony with love and compassion.

"Before I left to see you, we talked about you and whether I could or should disclose anything about this to you. Roberto said I could. I took him into our community in Assisi and immediately gave him food—soup, bread, some vegetables, fruit, and milk. I took him in to show him where the shower was because he looked like he hadn't bathed for quite some time. He appeared ill to me, so I convinced him to see one of the brothers involved in healthcare. He did see him and ordered some tests. He had gotten involved with the whole IV drug abuse scene and sold himself frequently to get heroin and cocaine but even more to eat. He often had to rummage through garbage to find something partly edible. He was at the point of taking his own life but chose to wander from place to place blindly, and that's how we bumped into each other. I believe God gave him some instinct to find where to find help. "

Dr. Vitali probed deeper, "You said he had some tests done. What were they? Were they normal if he allowed you to discuss this with me?"

"Roberto looked ashamed when he came out of the physician's office. He told me that he had HIV and hepatitis. I just held his hand as he patted it. Visions of Mama dying from AIDS and pneumonia frightened me. Fortunately, however, his white blood cells—no, it was his shoot! I don't remember the name of them." Luca listened carefully and said, "You mean his T cells or T lymphocytes? Is that what you were trying to remember?"

"Yes… that's it. Roberto's T cells were not too low, but the virus levels were high," Tony said. "Papa, do you think you can help him…please?"

His Papa agreed, "We will do our best to help him. Good medications treat a lot better than when your Mama died. Of course, Dr. Rossi and

I will do our best. There wasn't anything working that well until the mid-1990s.

"Thank you…O…thank you so much, Papa! Although we haven't had sex since he moved away almost 15 years ago, he wanted me to get tested, which I did. All of those results were negative. Thank the Lord, the blessed one," Tony told his father.

Papa asked, "When will I see Roberto again for his care? I may think it wise for Dr. Rossi to evaluate him since I know him through you and he is close like family, but I can see him for any other problem or just socially with you." Luca told Tony, then started downing his breakfast.

"Well," Tony said, "I brought him with me. He's a bit shy around medical folk but trusts you, Papa. I told him about that night we read Psalm 139 together, and Toni got all choked up. Just a minute," Tony uttered as he walked out the door. "Psst, Roberto…hey, Roberto, come here. Papa would like to see you."

Roberto hesitated, then came into Luca's room. Roberto walked toward Dr. Vitali's bed with head held down, covered with midnight sky, black and long curls. His skin was dark from the sun and the tan he always seemed to have, and he had on a patterned shirt too oversized for him and tight, slightly torn jeans with well-used sneakers. "Hello, Dr. Vitali. Are you feeling better?" he asked, standing ten feet away from Luca. "I hope so! Tony was telling me you had a heart attack. Good people like you shouldn't get heart attacks. You're too young to be having that kind of stuff happening." Then streams ran down his cheeks, and he had a scruffy black beard.

"Come here, son…yes, since you lost your Dad, I can take care of you like a father, where I can. You're family to us, Roberto. We are here to help you." Waving him to come over, Luca gave Roberto a big manly hug, and Orazio as he came over to the bedside. He kissed both of their foreheads. "If it is OK with you, I want you to see my physician partner, Dr. Primo Rossi. He is the best in the business of making infections better. Though very kind and compassionate, he can maintain any doctor's professional distance. Tony and I can be the educated family you need for support now." Turning the hospital call light on and handing them plenty of money, Luca instructed Roberto and Tony to grab something to eat in the town square. They left him by himself until the nurse retrieved the call.

"Yes, Dr. Vitali. How may I assist you?" Nurse Ibrahim, who had cared for him the night before, said." Oh, hello. It is good to see you again. Is the cardiology team rounding soon? Since last night, I haven't heard anything and am wondering when I can be discharged?" Luca answered.

She replied, "No, they haven't rounded on this unit today yet. But Dr. Rossi and Dr. Isabella Barone wanted to stop by when you were up. I will let them know you are up now, OK?"

He nodded and answered, "Yes, that would be great. Thank you!" He kept thinking about what Primo, Tony, and Roberto had said about working too hard, being too young to have heart issues and worried that he was making an early grave for himself because of his overworking. He worried about that, too, now that he had a heart issue. "But there are people that need me, right? Or am I as expendable as the next guy?" he thought aloud and was startled by Primo and Dr. Barone when they entered the room.

"Well, how are you doing? Are you ready to go home with us now?" Dr. Barone asked.

"I am not sure how to answer that. Orazio, known as Tony, and his friend Roberto were here about an hour ago. I want to get out of here, but I should wait for their return," he said.

Primo said, "Call them on their cellphones."

Luca interrupted, "I can't do that. Neither of the guys has a cell phone; it would surprise me if they did. Anyway, I don't have their numbers if they do have some. I only seldom get to talk to Tony. He works at a monastery in Assisi. I wouldn't know if Roberto had one either."

Dr. Barone stated, "When they return, let us know. One of the residents wrote your discharge orders, and I will have one of my colleagues see you in a couple of weeks and sign you up for cardiac rehab three times a week. OK, we'll see you when you get home—our home. Call us if you need assistance in getting home.

"OK, I will do that. Thanks for everything. See you when I get home. Bye-bye," Luca saluted. With the IV still in place, he was waiting to have it pulled and to bathe. Dr. Vitali strolled to the window feeling better than he had over the last few months. He sighed heavily as Primo and Isabella were primed for marriage. Should he find a place of his own? What about dating so late in life? How was the puzzle of his life going to be worked out? He decided to move out and find a place alone but shook his head, saying, "I am not ready to date anyone else. Anna-Claire was enough to fill three lifetimes brimming with love. I've got my God, work, and children—what more do I need?" As he was in discussion with himself, Nurse Ibrahim walked in.

"It is noon, and the medical resident has written your discharge orders. Let me pull out the IV and check your groin sight for any bleeding after you've stood up now for a little bit, Dr. Vitali," the nurse insisted.

"Everything looks great, so you're ready to go at your leisure after signing these discharge papers, and your home medicines come up from the pharmacy." Luca lay back in the hospital bed and let her do her duties. She looked at the groin site where the cardiac catheterization was performed and freed him from his IV.

"Well, that could take another week," Luca joked and lively chuckled. The nurse smiled broadly. "You've got that right, doctor!" she said.

"It will be good to take a shower. Could you please bring some fresh towels and soap for now? On second thought, I'll wait to do that when I get home. Thank you. And best of luck to you and in your studies at Columbia. What will you do when medical school is finished? What type of physician do you want to be?" the doctor asked.

The nurse replied, "I am not sure at this time, but probably internal medicine…just to be a generalist. I want to return to Karachi, where my brothers and mother live. I want to give e back to my family and country when I finish."

"That sounds very noble of you. I wish you all the best truly," Luca said approvingly. "Goodbye, and do take good care of yourself!" Roberto and Tony returned, happy to see Luca out of bed and ready to leave. "I want to call Vani and Alessandro before they leave and tell them where we'll be. Maybe we could meet at Primo's, where I live now, and have dinner late."

"Excuse me, doctor," Roberto earnestly said. "If I can be so bold, you just had a heart attack. You don't have to entertain us. You need your rest and to relax. Tony and I can find our way around Milano. You have been so kind to me that we could not impose on supper."

Tony agreed, was no longer comfortable around wealth or privilege, and cared so much that his father would be OK. "Papa, let us take care of you; get things for you. We will do that for you need to relax. You're always bones to the grindstone. It's time for us to care for you. You are your own worst patient!" the son of Vitali said in a humorous tone.

"Both you and Roberto relax and talk. I can go to the market and bring some things to make supper at your place tonight. Both of you need to get well. I love you both. Please let me know. Where are you living now?"

"OK. I am currently living with Primo in his place in Brera. Here are the address and my number and his. In fact, why don't we head there now, and you can get your bearings around the city? We will take a taxi there, and I will give you my cellphone if you need us."

"Now, let me call Vani and Alessandro and tell them where to meet us, just a minute," Luca said. "Ciao, Vani, are you and Alessandro planning to come to Milano? I am now being discharged and going to Dr. Rossi's home."

"Ciao, Grandpapa, it is me, Alessandro. Yes, my Dad and I are coming to see you, and we should be there in an hour. He is driving, so I will let him know." Immediately, without asking anything more, Alessandro inadvertently hung up the phone.

"Is anybody there? Hello, anybody there?" Luca asked, but the phone was almost out of charge, so he did not call him back. So, Roberto, Tony, and Papa left the hospital and quickly found a taxi to Primo's place. "It doesn't look like anyone is at home," Luca said bluntly. "I have a key. Here we go to the place."

Shaken by the Primo's home's opulence, Tony said, "Papa, do you think it is all right to…I mean, did you talk to Dr. Rossi about us coming? We could find a hostel or anything else. We don't mean to intrude."

"Yes," Luca answered. "He knows all about it, and I asked him to see Roberto as you seemed to say it would be good for him to see a specialist. Primo is the best doctor I know. I want you to stay in town until Roberto's medicine is started and see how he tolerates it."

"Are you sure? Really? I don't have any money to buy medicine or see a doctor," Roberto reluctantly admitted, but the doctor reassured him that he would care for his care's financial end. "Oh, forever, thank you. I don't know what I would have done."

"My area is on the ground level, and there are some rooms on the lower level that I am sure you can use," Luca said cordially. "Why don't you both wash up? Your brother and nephew should be here fairly soon. It must have been some time since you have seen Vani and his boy."

"It has been a while…probably 18 months or so. I haven't seen them since your last big birthday celebration," Tony replied.

The younger men headed downstairs, and Luca headed for the shower to freshen up for the evening. All the family talk made him miss Anna-Claire.

CHAPTER ELEVEN :

ARIA'S, VANI'S, AND ALESSANDRO'S DILEMMAS

◇◇

Aria's life appeared to be an undisturbed life living in Italy. However, inside, it was fraught with fear and anxiety. She was drawn to the adventurous life of an environmental scientist. She could be anywhere. What if she was gone, and Papa needed her comfort? He might have some dreaded disease from which there was no cure, as AIDS with her mom had been.

She believed by being a good…no… a great ecologist and environmentalist, she could fill in the void in Luca's life that Anna-Claire had done. She wanted the limelight attention. Aria loved her Papa more than anyone else, and disappointing him in any way seemed unthinkable and untenable. Her excellent marks in school made finding a college or university anywhere in Europe and around the world easy. If she stayed behind at home, Aria thought, "I do not want to disappoint Papa by not going ahead and pursuing a career in some form of ecology, which is my dream, like what Mama had. It is important to me to fill that spot in some way. Papa and I need to discuss this as soon as possible. I will run it by Vani first—I think."

At that moment, Sandro and I entered the home to get cleaned up from a hard day working at the farm. I brought Alessandro (Sandro) with me. Sandro was 17 and was usually bright and cheerful, but tonight he was different. He gazed outside the window and was silent. His animation appeared to be deflated…his energy was gone.

Aria was in the kitchen making lasagna for the family: her dad, brother, nephew, and herself. I came into the kitchen after showering and getting out of his sweaty, grubby clothes. "Hey, Aria, you seem distracted about something important. Did you meet your dream guy today or get engaged? Ha! Ha! "I chuckled. "What's on your mind? You and Sandro look so distant tonight. I can understand why my son is upset with me. But you…Have I done something wrong or hurt you, Aria?

"No, no. Not at all. Just the opposite. I need to talk to you about something important. I wanted to do that before our father comes home in an hour or so." Arias strongly said.

I replied, "When has Papa ever been home at the time he said he would? I bet he won't be here until double the time. Sure. I want to chat with you for a while, too. What's up? What did you want to talk about?"

"Let me get this in the oven before we do that," Aria stated, "You and Sandro must be famished after working on the farm all day in this hot weather. Just a moment."

" OK. That's fine." I agreed. After grabbing an orange or two and some water, "I will sit and rest in the living room and watch the news. Get me when you discuss whatever is on your mind."

I hadn't been watching Alessandro but reasoned that he must have walked while Aria cooked dinner. I reached for the most comfortable chair the room had to offer and sat on it. The minute I sat down, my eyelids dropped, and I dozed off. Immediately, I began dreaming.

First, I dreamt about my time in England at Oxford University. The rough beginning days in school…initially about my loneliness. I was mocked and usually got into a brawl, so I took the gut punch, bit my tongue, and then let it go. However, women were attracted by my good looks, and foreign accent, and generally mild demeanor. He dreamt of the pubs he used to go to in London.

The affable Ken Morrison (who had been my roommate) became my companion and confidante. Although, in the dream, Ken was at the bar, slumped over it with bloody and smelly clothes. They smelled like the odor of an embalmed corpse. It smelled like formaldehyde and cologne, like Papa's aroma on the first date with Anna-Claire when Vani was conceived.

The aroma of Luca's shirt turned into a PTSD episode and became a nightmare. Vani walked up to Ken and tapped him on the shoulder. However, this time, Ken's body was cold and pale., but he was still bleeding until his blood could be seen flooding up the pub to the cracked and shard-ridden mirrors surrounding him. In the broken glass, I saw the blood in the ocean on that fateful day of Ken's death. I impregnated one of the young "ladies of the night" before the brawl with the neo-Nazis. The barn where I held my best friend as he died.

Also, I visualized Sandro's birth, the woman from England to Italy, and I saw my baby boy for the first time. About a month later, early Saturday morning, Sandro's mother snuck out and left Alessandro with me without speaking a word. I was now Sandro's only hope to avoid becoming an orphan. I saw Alessandro on a ventilator in the distance as if in a fog. The dream ended when a physician rammed an endotracheal tube (ET) down my throat. Aria tapped on my shoulder. I woke up choking with blurry eyes. Afterward, I stumbled into the kitchen, put my head in the sink, and turned on the cold water to get going. After shaking off my nightmare, I raised my voice and told Aria only bits and pieces.

After hearing my dream, Aria interrupted, saying, 'Papa will be here soon, and the lasagna will be done shortly. What should I do about leaving Italy and studying environmental science at the University of Queensland in Australia, where I have already been accepted and have merit scholarships waiting for me if I desire? "

I stated, "I am not the best person to ask about school overseas because of my experience at Oxford University in England and all that followed there and here. I smudged the name of the Vitalis across Europe, and Papa intervened on my behalf. He is the best and kindest man I know and a great father. Papa is always in your corner, no matter how far you dug yourself into a hole. He's, I guess, like Jesus, whom he told me was his life example. Always with you no matter how far you've strayed…He is there and won't leave us in our distress. I love Papa and don't know what I would have done without his company, wisdom, guidance and love." I stopped. My eyes suddenly filled with tears, but I did not cry or sob but felt an indescribable emotion. All the children of my family felt an intense bond with our father, I took a deep breath and sighed heavily. Clearing my throat, I said, "I know one thing for sure: how proud he is of you and would want you to open your wings and start flying to where your heart and mind lead you,"

"Thank you, Vani., I needed to hear that today. I think I am ready to talk with Papa about Australia and why that is the perfect start of my college," said Aria. "Well, let's get ready for supper. Sandro, go wash your hands and come join us." But Aria and I heard no reply, which was shocking to us.

I had not kept track of where my son went that evening. Simultaneously, we both panicked but tried to put our heads together to figure out where he might be. I searched the rooms in the house upstairs and downstairs without any luck while Aria called and looked outside. There was no evidence of where Alessandro might be, except I noticed his bike was missing. It was pretty unusual for Sandro not to sit down to a meal with his family, especially when his favorite meal was being served--- Aria's Lasagna.

Where could he be? It was getting close to 9:30 PM, and Papa and Sandro were nowhere to be found. They tried calling and texting Alessandro and his grandfather on their cell phones many times. There was no reply from either after a dozen calls. What the hell is going on? Frightened by their absence, Aria and I took to each other's car and drove in opposite directions to find Papa and Sandro. Neither of us thought of going to Papa's clinic---the worry had gotten the best of us. We were not thinking not planning out a stepwise search.

Sandro had called his grandpa to talk face-to-face. "Ciao, Grandpa. This is Sandro. I must be alone and have some undisturbed time to talk with you. I don't want my father to be here or involved in our conversation. You know what I mean, at least not this time. I need desperately to talk with you this evening before I do something stupid that I will regret afterward," Sandro was slurring his words after guzzling a bottle and a half of red wine. Luca, his grandfather, had never heard him so desperate, insistent, or intoxicated.

Dr. Vitali picked up on the alarm and urgency of his grandson's plea. "Sure, Sandro. Do you want me to pick you up somewhere, or maybe you remember how to get to where I work? Do you remember?" Luca said with the same gentle and calming voice he used when talking to Tony about his love for Roberto years before and Vani's allegations.

Alessandro shook his head to wake up; although he was dizzy and his eyesight was blurry and coughing, he said, "I do remember Grandpa. I will be there as soon as I can. Maybe 10-15 minutes. Is that OK with you?"

"Sure thing. Sandro. I will be here, and we can discuss whatever is on your mind. Sometimes that's best." stated Luca. Could he be that helpful to his teenage grandson tonight? The doctor pondered what could be so urgent that Sandro pressed to see him this evening. At the same time, he was attempting to figure out what might be wrong. Luca saw his grandson riding into the clinic's entrance from his laboratory window.

Luca immediately descended the staircases at record speed, getting short of breath and nauseated when he reached the bottom where Sandro was. He went out the clinic's door and greeted Alessandro. With furrowed brow but with his compassionate eyes, he spoke, "Come on in, Sandro. It is good to see you, which I haven't done for a while. Let's go to my laboratory workplace, and we won't be disturbed there."

"OK. Wherever you want, let's go. Grandpa, can you climb all these stairs? It seems like a long way up there." Sandro uttered. "Are you sure you can make it? We can talk wherever it's private and quiet, with just you and me." Luca insisted they climb the four staircases with steep steps leading to his office. So, when they got to the top, the doctor had to take some time to catch his breath and get his chest pain to go away before shuffling off to the lab. He was a little pale, but as he rested, the whole natural flush of his face returned.

"Are you OK, Grandpa.?" Alessandro probed." If you aren't, we can wait until you feel better tonight." Sandro insisted.

"Oh, that's nothing to worry about. It has happened to me a lot lately, and I guess it is because I am getting up there in years," the doctor stated confidently. Earnestly, looking intently, he questioned Sandro about what was bothering him. " I was surprised when you called. What is it, my friend?" (He often greeted even family members as his friends, no matter how old or young.) "You don't appear to be doing very well, Sandro. I am here to listen, and if you want my input, I will gladly give it if you ask me to."

Sandro's face blushed, and he cleared his throat. He did not feel the buzz of the wine anymore but felt more comfortable talking with the senior member of his family. "Well, Grandpa, my dad and I fought before coming to your place for dinner. He told me everything that happened to him when he was in England before I was born. I never knew he was accused of murdering his best friend on the same day when he f**ked a woman he had never met before while at that pub. No, that whorehouse!! Sorry, Grandpa, I cuss too much. I mean no disrespect. He got her pregnant. Yes, I was born a bastard nine months later!! On the same day, his best mate died in my dad's lap, all bloody and cold. Dad told me he was raped in prison in the UK and nearly died…on the same night! He told me you came and saved the day and his life.

My dad told me how you bailed him out and cared for him medically and legally. Then he left England and never returned, not knowing my mother was carrying me. It doesn't sound like he was around when I was born in that country. She eventually found him in Italy after I grew up in England without him for about a year. My mother, God knows her name, brought me from the UK to Italy. She just wanted to get paid what was due to her for my care in the first year. Then she disappeared, and all I had was my father; otherwise, I guess I would be in some orphanage somewhere or adopted or something like that,"

Then, Sandro punched his grandpa's desk, and his eyes flooded with tears rolling down his cheeks and chin. "Why didn't my dad tell me this until now? Then he told me he was sick with HIV, and I guess if my dad didn't take his medicines, he could die from AIDS. Damn! Not only did he tell me I was a bastard, but that he could die from the dreaded infection. He didn't call me a bastard. That's what I am! I am so f***king mad at him. He unloaded all this trash on me today,,,5 DAYS AWAY FROM MY BIRTHDAY ON SATURDAY! I don't know why he had to do that now!" Sandro questioned loudly.

Sandro continued, "I don't know what he'll unload on me next. I am scared, mad, and sad. All wrapped together. I don't know why he didn't tell me this before. Didn't he trust me, Grandpa? I feel like killing myself. You are the only one I can trust. And you are the one I trust in this world! What should…What can I do? There is no way out. I thought I would tell you I was planning to ride my bike over some cliff or something!" Then Sandro paused with a clenched fist and jaw but crying nonetheless. "I don't know what to do!"

"Hush now, Alessandro; first of all, I want you to know I love you deeply and know your dad does, too …Did you know I am privileged to be your grandfather? Thank you for reaching out to me and sharing your story. I have never felt or thought you were a "bastard" or "a mistake." You are a Vitali through and through and a beautiful part of this family. You are exceptional and my first grandson, the firstborn! Never say that about yourself anymore! Never! What you have told me is just between you and me and anyone else you want to tell. It is confidential… I do and will respect that. My dear boy, I know life has been cruel to you, and you feel hopeless. I can only imagine how difficult it is for you. Anybody would have similar feelings if they had similar things happen to them. That must be very painful! I am here for you. I do think we should go to the hospital together and make sure you are safe and find some relief., I will stay with you tonight as long as you want me to or until the hospital's regulations say I must leave. Does that sound OK to you? I do need to tell your dad and aunt that we are together and safe. That's all I need to say to them. I won't give any details unless you permit me. Don't worry about me talking to them. Let's go to the Emergency Room and figure out what is best for you and find someone, some professional, that you can spill your guts out to t with until you feel and are safe."

Sandro's face was reddish-purple, and he was sobbing uncontrollably. He hugged Papa tightly and would be hard to pull apart. "Yeah, we can go to the hospital," he said with a hesitatingly quivering voice, "but stay with me, PLEASE!! Don't ever let me go! Don't leave me, Grandpa. Don't let me go!! Don't…" he blurted out desperately. Catching his breath but still clinging tightly, he cleared his throat and wiped his eyes. This scene was distantly familiar to Dr. Viali. This scenario was typical within the context of standing up against the bullies in high school for other kids.

Aria and I headed in the same direction, checking out hospitals' ERs. Maybe that was the dream I had told Aria hours before. All I could see in my head was that Sando was seriously injured somewhere, and it was my fault because I argued with Sandro before coming over for dinner. Maybe all that blood he saw in his nightmare while sitting in the comfy living room chair was Alessandro's. He felt that even more intensely, remembering the ICU hospital bed in the distance when he awoke.

Aria felt some weird guilt about leaving for Australia. Perhaps she was needed more at home. Bringing up the subject of leaving Europe to go to the ends of the earth released some horrible plague on her family. She shook the emotion off as superstitious, telling herself it was all in her mind. However, the missing family members caught her off guard and unprepared. The conflicting thoughts were that her dreams of being the environmentalist she wanted to be were being flushed down the toilet. Visions of that role in life and the world stemmed back to childhood. What was happening??? She choked back tears and turned her face to the side to be the "strong one" here.

Besides, Luca was missing, too. She surmised that her brother-in-law was pushing himself too far off the edge. I was in deep distress, not knowing what to do or where to go. Their Papa's good friend Primo would know. Aria scrambled through her cellphone's contact list, hoping she would find his number. She called Dr. Possi immediately/

"Dr. Rossi! Ciao. This is Aria Vitali. You know. Vani and I are calling from Milano, and we last saw Papa or Sandro a few hours ago!

Something horrible might have happened to both of them! Do you know where Papa might be? Is he there with you?"

"Calm down, Aria. And you too, Vani. I am sure that it is alright. Take a slow, deep breath. It will help with your anxiety. Perhaps your dad took Sandro out for a special or surprise birthday meal together since it's Sandro's birthday this Saturday. He had said something like that a week or two ago. Maybe that's all it is," Primo spoke confidently to decrease the panic, but he was more concerned than he let on to be. "I wouldn't worry too much about it. If they're not back with you in the morning, we can do a more thorough search with the aid of the police. I think it all will be OK, maybe like playing a game together or talking to each other about other things going on in your life. I am being trite or don't care. Things will turn out fine. As for me, I am in Geneva at a conference so I will not be available until Tuesday. Ciao."

On the call, Primo had little intensity that Aria and I were looking for tonight. Dr. Rossi said he and Papa had gone through scores of crises together

CHAPTER TWELVE:

ALESSANDRO'S ARRIVAL IN PSYCH PURGATORY

◇◇◇

Dr. Vitali was bent on helping Sandro's deal with my portfolio of tragedy and rescue in his merry-go-round of crises. That night, the echoes and mirages of him and me were too much, too sharp to absorb. Sandro's head was spinning out of reasonable control, and his thinking was, at best, foggy. His discussion with his grandfather eased the shipwreck of his talk with me hours before. In Sandro's eyes, Papa had this way about him through his own life of pain and joy---seeming to waltz over every tempest and storm. Grandpa's intoxicating voice was so captivating that Sandro's fear and anguish, which had held him so tightly just a few moments ago, now abated. His weeping subsided, and his energy returned.

However, in Dr. Vitali's wisdom, they headed out, found some eatery, and walked shoulder-to-shoulder to the mental health ward where Papa worked. This stroll together reassured them that this rekindled kinship would remain (as essential to Papa as it was to his grandson). While admitted, the two of them could see each other daily. Sandro counted on it...with his life, and Luca always kept his word.

Sandro was led into the psychiatric holding room and waited for the psychiatric provider's assessment. "Grandpa, were you ever in a psych ward before? I mean like this. Did you ever need help sorting out your feelings and thinking? Were you ever suicidal?" Sandro asked.

"No, Sandro. Although there were times when I thought my life would surely end or I would surely end my life. That may be a common way for everyone," Papa replied." I was at that place when your grandmother died. But I had to feed, clothe, and bathe your uncle, aunts, and Dad. It was a joy to raise them despite my missing her. And now, I'm here with you, my boy, and I wouldn't trade the world for this time I get to spend with you. Right now, you are my only grandchild and grandson! Nothing takes the place of the ones you love. Like you, yes, like you!"

Their conversation ended abruptly when the mental health provider called, "Alessandro Vitali! Alessandro Vitali!!" Sandro let go of clutching Dr. Vitali's arm. "Goodbye, Grandpa. I'll miss you. Tell Dad I love him! Please., please. I really do, and I'm sorry!" Then Sandro went off with the case worker. Dr. Vitali stressed to the staff the need for Sandro's admission. The doctor left to get his car nearby.

Out of the blue, Aria and I saw and met Papa on the street. Shocked that we were not at home but had been anxiously searching for him, he emphatically exclaimed," What are you two doing here? What brought you here? Why here?"

Aria and I were amazed to see Papa was well. The three of us climbed into Papa's car and headed toward home. Aria was crying and trembling, but I had cheery-red cheeks and a huge grin, so relieved that we had found each other. We were delighted to be together, so much so that Sandro was only mentioned about halfway home. Then Papa slammed on the brakes. "Wait a moment! I didn't tell you, but Sandro is on the Pieta floor getting help dealing with your conversation today, Your dad before you came for dinner. You and he need some family counseling and mending your relationship. You and he need all the support you can get. I know that Aria and I would love to be that for you. Right, Aria?"

"Oh, yeah, for sure!" Aria agreed." I wonder, though, what was going through Sandro's mind. What affected him the most in your story, Vani? What do you think?"

I was looking out of the car into the street when he saw the boy with the candle and heard his voice chime, "Remember.". Remember what? I thought I saw the same boy that Papa did after dropping off me and himself into Uncle Romeo and Anita's care many years ago. Remember that or when Ken died in his arms? Remember how Papa had rescued him after his gang rape in jail? Or when Sandro and I would play games or soccer with each other as Sandro matured? No, I remembered my lack of praise and gratitude for Sandro working hard with me on the farm daily. Yes, that should be foremost in my mind...appreciating my son's companionship and the joy of having a son like Sandro. Yes, that was it! Yes. Sandro himself! I should remember him.

Suddenly, I cried out," Stop! Stop the car now!" The car shrieked to stop, and then I bolted out of the car and darted back to the hospital as fast as he could at 11:00 PM. I said no good byes. However, I first chased after the boy with the candle, softly singing, "Remember." But again, that child disappeared without a trace. After a few minutes of pursuit, I changed direction and aimed straight at the hospital where Sandro was. It was the right time. Yep, it's the right time!

I ran past the Security police in the hallway to the ward where his boy was. I reached the security door, and the Security Guard grabbed me by the scruff of my neck and lifted me off the ground. I demanded to be let in to see my son, saying, "I'm Dr. Vitali's son. Dr. Luca Vitali. You hear me??"

"Quiet! Quiet! I am taking you, and you're out of here. You're not welcome to come here. Get out of here!" Strong as I was and in the adrenaline rush to find my son, I threw off the Security Guard and again started banging on the door. "Let me in, damn it. Now!"

At that very moment, the intercom rang out." Code Yellow 4th floor Unit 7 alpha !! Again, Code Yellow 4th floor Unit & alpha! Immediately, a herd of guards came to the locked Psychiatry Ward and tackled me to the floor. Fortunately, to my rescue again, like Papa had done in the past, came running and panting down the hallway where the operator had called the Code Yellow.Dr. Vitali knew it was the Psych Ward's unit number and reckoned I was trying feverishly to get into see Sandro.

Sandro heard my voice and ran to see through the small window where he was to see what was happening. Cheek and nose smudged against the windowpane; he could glimpse what was happening. It was Dad! It was his Dad's Dad coming to liberate him. Sandro's heart was beating so fast that he collapsed in the mental health corridor, and the psychiatric staff quickly came to his side. They lifted him to the department's couch and gave him a glass of cold water. He fainted from the excitement.

During the mayhem of the moment, Sandro's Grandpa fell and hit his head against the wall, eager to come to my aid. The guards recognized it was a physician they had seen before and let Vani go. Immediately, he rushed to Papa.

Aria was in the background, pale and crying. Oh, what a scene it was, like something you'd see in the movies! It was a circus extraordinaire! But Sandro saw how much his father loved and cared about him. Although, he and I knew we had to work to get to know each other on a whole new basis. It was good that Alessandro saw how much Papa loved me too. He was amazed at how deeply his Grandpa cared for so many people. From the doctor's sickest patient to his father and aunt, he showed kindness to him just a few hours ago. Sandro's suicidal ideation and plan subsided, but his eyes were full of tears. He thought pain between two people if someone cared and loved each member from the outside. There was something he had not disclosed to anybody.

It was time to let complete strangers in a psychiatrist and her psychological assistants. The psychiatrist was female in her late 30s. She was different from any doctor or woman he had ever met. Her compassion was clearly evident on her face. Aqua-blue eyes that could see right through you. You could not escape her sight or gaze. Her voice was soft and calming, with a particular strength from authority and humility. She was not from Italy or of Italian descent. Her family lived on a farm in Lancaster, Pennsylvania. in the United States. However, no one could differentiate her from any other Italian born on the Italian-Swiss border in northern Italy when she spoke Italian. It was only later that she disclosed that information to Sandro.

Her name was Dr. Amy Caren Troyer. To Sandro, she possessed that quality of care and nurture he had always wanted in a mother. Here she was.his chance in a lifetime! Being blonde and fair-skinned with no jewelry or make-up and somewhat chubby but attractive., She was shorter than he was. Her clothes were plain and not the elaborate Versace clothes he was used to seeing around his Grandpa's clinic. It caught him and many others off-guard.

"Sandro, are you OK? Let's sit down and talk. Would you like coffee, a soft drink, water or something?" she said welcomely.

"I'll take a Coke if you have it." She opened up the bottle of Coke and poured the drink into a plastic cup. Whenever the patients wanted some soda, she and the psych assistants were meticulous about discarding or giving any beverage in a can or glass. The doctors and staff knew that glass had to be hazard-free. Glass and sharp metal were some things, by experience, not to be around in case one of the teens used it as a weapon toward themselves or others. It was fresh in their memory because it happened not too long ago.

Sandro was understandably distracted by all the commotion with me. He was also frightened by being alone in a scary place like he figured this place could be. Past all of Sandro's demographics, Dr. Troyer began her questioning initially slowly with an almost monotone feel; afterward, she started her psychiatric assessment.

"Sandro, what's on your mind? Why did you come to the hospital? What is the purpose of being here? What are you expecting, and what goals do you hope to achieve during your stay in this unit?"

Sandro hesitated and stuttered unintelligibly." what did you say, Sandro?" Tears ran down the young man's cheeks unabashedly. He realized no other woman had ever taken the time to care for him. Like a baby on a mother's breast, he sucked in every kind word and compassionate look from Dr. Troyer's face. Her slowly deliberate but femininely nudged questions she asked, he answered in amazement. Hard questions seemed easy to Sandro.

The same type of intoxication and "hypnosis" the young man sensed had happened to him two hours before with Grandpa. This emotional magnetism was the same with Dr. Troyer. This mystery had its key discovered, right? Why now, and what was the connection between the two? She felt like family! She could be family. She was like, he thought, the description of his grandmother he heard so much about from Grandpa. But he never met her. What on earth was happening to him? This person was not his mother. Surely not! Who is this psychiatrist anyway? She must be part of his family, or did she cast a spell on him?

Sandro, who lay on the ward's couch, suddenly jumped to his feet feeling confused in the good sense of the word. He relaxed and stood in the presence of this physician. "Doctor," Sandro started," I am baffled. Who are you? I know you, but I can't place where I've met you before! It feels like I am dreaming, but I am awake. I know it's not the alcohol or the drugs I downed."

Curiously, he vacillated from being totally at peace to freaked out. Why was she so magnetic to him? He knew she was there when he was ready to throw himself off the bridge. She was there saying urgently, "Let's go see your Grandpa. Come on, come on down, Sandro." When he got down, she was gone! Only a small child was singing mysteriously, "Remember. Remember." This woman and child were trying to keep the fabric of this family from ripping. Divine? Angelic? This scene was like when Grandpa returned to the hospital when Grandma was sick. Also, his Dad saw him only minutes before he ran to the hospital to get close to Sandro.

Following that experience, he hoped the darkness and loathsome lonely existence of drinking and snorting were gone. He wouldn't return, he promised himself. Unlike other doctors on the unit and psychiatric personnel, she curiously went to her locker and pulled out her Bible.

"Sandro, you feel you are not being heard," the doctor said. Sandro nodded his head affirmatively. "It felt like she was reading my mind," he thought. Unbelievable!"

She said, "You're not alone. I have, at times I have thought likewise. Sometimes, you are shy about your family because they are different than everyone else's. Here in Italy, you will find a few Mennonites, sometimes called Anabaptists. Yes, it is unusual. We are Christians with a long heritage of living in Switzerland and Southern Germany and have been persecuted almost all our history. If you would like to talk about it later, we can. But now it's your time, Sandro."

With his brow wrinkled, he said, "Why the Bible? Dad and I aren't very religious. I don't believe in any god. But if you want, you can tell me what you want. I trust you. I do not know why. I feel safe with you when I am with you. So, what would be helpful and not preachy?"

"I am sure you never have heard this from a preacher. A king wrote this when he felt lonely and wasn't being seen or heard. His family was in shambles. Who, when he was alone, made sense of it all? Nobody hears or sees me. Sound familiar? The Psalm says, "Lord, you have probed and know me. You know when I sit down and when I sit up. You discern my inclinations from afar. You scrutinize my daily activities.

You are so familiar with all my ways that before I speak even a word, Lord, you know about it already...You fashioned my being; you knit me together in my mother's womb. I thank you. I am awesomely made... my bones were not hidden from you when I was made in secret, intricately woven in the depths of the earth. Your eyes could see me as an embryo, but in your book, all my days were written; my days had been shaped before any of them existed, and it goes on from there". (Psalm 139. The Complete Jewish Bible)

"Oh, yeah. I heard some of it from my Uncle Tony a long time ago. He told me Grandpa read it to him when he had troubles during high school. I guess I am about the same age.," he replied to the doctor.

"It sounds like you and your Grandpa and Uncle Tony are pretty close, huh?" she said in a positive tone.

"That is true, but I don't see them very often. Grandpa is a doctor and a really busy man taking care of patients and doing research. Uncle Tony lives with many monks in Assisi and doesn't have a car of his own drive. He doesn't talk all that much, but he listens closely like nobody I've ever met," he informed her with a sigh.

"How about your Dad? He cares a lot about you. Does he? How do you feel about him?" the female psychiatrist queried.

"I don't know right now. I am mad at my Dad for covering up and lying about his life. Like I wasn't good enough to trust and couldn't understand it. Then, he told me he had viral infections he could die from, and they swim around in his blood. I am sorry, you know, his sperm. F**k, f**K, f**k.! Hell! I don't want him to die. Then I would be truly an orphan, a bastard child...Oops! Grandpa recently told me I shouldn't talk about myself like that. I will not sit around to watch him die and be an orphan. What kind of God would do that? That is to be the end. I have worried about his crap ever since I was a little kid. When he dies, I'll die. Without him, then? Who'll always be my friend, joke around like Dad, and be there when I screw up? And I don't know what I'd do. You might as well put a nail in my casket, too. We are a team, so why haven't you told me until now? I don't know how to help him except stay out of his way."

After several days, the unit released Sandro from the hospital. His Grandpa and I were joyfully outside the ward. His Dad was the first to run, hug, and hold Sandro against his chest in gratitude. Grandpa joined the hugging huddle, also.

Despite Dr. Troyer's absence, both son and father managed to reconcile. Sandro watched me like a hawk and kept looking for anything that looked like an infection might be brewing. Likewise, I gently scrutinized cues concerning Sandro's mental health issues. Together, they blocked any death or disease from their household.

CHAPTER THIRTEEN:

SANDRO'S PURGATORY INTO THE FLAMES

◇◇◇

Like almost every other guy in their late teens and young adulthood where Sandro lived, they experimented with drugs and alcohol and had sex early in their youth. I was no exception. Alessandro (Sandro) was no different from the rest of them either. By the time he was admitted to the psychiatric unit, he was, at least in part, becoming more dependent on all three. Sandro was best friends with Giacobbe Cavaliere.

Giacobbe, sometimes called by his last name, was tall and exceptionally strong but not nearly as handsome as Sandro. However, he had the most beautiful emerald green eyes. He worked out daily with weights and less with cardiovascular exercise; however, his best friend, Sandro, could quickly run circles around him.

Giacobbe needed academic acumen and intellectual training to pursue meaningful and productive employment. He had excessive inertia regarding work or school until Sandro Sandro's quick wit and vitality captivated his attention. Sandro's diligence in his studies amazed him. Giacobbe never wanted to be "intelligent" until he saw this characteristic in his friend. However, he had a covert and cunning way of overcoming social hurdles. Their traits unconventionally complemented each other.

They prodded each other for the higher spot when it came to risk. This was their modus operandi, their MO. Neither I nor Cavaliere's parents knew of the boys' whereabouts in their dangerous territories, which may be trying the newest dope, gambling, or the company dozen hookers in the red-light district. The boy's exploits remained under wraps but became more precarious as time passed. They went to places of ill-repute scores of times, mainly on the weekends. They usually wore protection with sexual activity, but once they forgot as they were heading out for an evening of unbridled pleasure. This time, they brought only one condom between them.

Sandro brought the only one but wanted his best friend to have protection. So, they flipped a coin, and Sandro lost the bet and this night's "protection," but Sandro halted and said, "Giacobbe, go ahead and have fun. I've got to think this out. I must figure out what I've got to do. Dad told me the truth about how and where I was conceived and stuff like that. He told me that his best friend was murdered that night, and it appeared to some people that Dad was at fault. My Dad's no murderer, especially of his buddy! It happened during a brawl in a pub where his friend got stabbed. He went through hell because of it. Grandpa came to his rescue, but Grandpa ransomed Dad to get released from jail in the UK. He had good defense lawyers, and he was found not guilty. Fortunately, a bystander in the bar testified that Dad was innocent and pinned the blame on one of the other men in the fight, and that man was charged and got a second-degree murder charge. Other things happened to him in jail, but that's a talk for a different time. Go on and be safe. I'll see you tomorrow."

With his massive, folded arms and staring angrily, his captivating green eyes nearly paralyzed Sandro. Over and over, Giacobbe kept urging and spurring him to come. He retorted, "That was then. This is now. Your Dad is your Dad and not you. Nothing terrible is going to happen tonight. If, for some reason, things get out of control, I'll take care of it. Yeah, for both of us. Come on, Sandro. Forget those thoughts. We can toss a coin again if you'd like. If you win the bet, I will go there without a rubber. Come on; nothing will happen to us differently tonight than any other night." He took a deep breath and sighed while annoyingly glared at his friend the whole time.

Sandro was almost persuaded to succumb to this intense peer pressure and sexual cravings. However, he felt a gentle voice reminding him of the Psalm he had heard from people he trusted and respected most at least twice in his life. Giacobbe kept provoking him to reconsider his actions. For the first time in Sandro's and Cavaliere's friendship, he said emphatically, "No! I'm not going with you! If you don't have the courtesy to see why I'm not coming, Then hell with you! Then you don't know me! No! I'm not going"" Tony turned away and began returning to our place.

Taken back by the fervor and determination of his friend's refusal, he shook his head, spat on the ground, and not saying another word, he resumed walking toward the red-light district. He vanished from sight into the twilight of that spine-chilling night. Sandro headed back home.

Out of the blue, that mysterious young boy came into view and softly sang, "Remember. Remember! "Both Dad and Grandpa saw him during some tough times. It was Sandro's turn now, with the crooning youngster holding a solitary brightly lit candle. This time, the child did not disappear from Sandro's view. The two walked home together as a younger brother or a bonded elementary schoolmate would. As they reached the front door's threshold, the younger lad looked into Sandro's eyes, handed him the candle he always had, whispered like a breeze or echo to Sandro, and said, crescendoing," Remember. Remember. Remember. Yes. Remember!" After his last articulation and giving Sandro the candle, this mysterious little friend, like a mime, sat down on a bench adjacent to Vani's and Sandro's place. Sandro would have encouraged him to come inside, but it was all too apparent that the youngster wanted to reside outside the home, gently gazing at the people inside.

This calming scene was aborted by an explosion and a news flash on the television. The commotion was about a loud reverberation, a flame spiraling into the sky, and smoke billowing heavenward, precisely where he was going with his buddy, Giacobbe, the hour before! Sandro's complexion went from his dark tan to the whiteness of a white porcelain doll. He shook uncontrollably. What happened to his friend and the other so-called patrons he always went with nearly every night during the summer? The discharge police and other investigators determined it was a meth lab that caught on fire. His fright dramatically and maybe life increased when he saw the charred body of his friend being carted off in an ambulance. Could artificial means of life support, like a ventilator, save his closest friend? Could he be seen by medical people in time to get life support and avoid death like Ken did fifteen years before?

Sandro realized he had been saved from this catastrophe and that the only thing that stopped in a visible realm was the absence of one condom! These small voices encouraging him not to proceed were an enigma, and then the "what ifs" poured into his mind. What if Vani had not relayed his story, for whatever reason, including shame, about the time and place his son was conceived? Or about what had happened to Ken dying in his father's arms, or about the trauma he experienced in jail due to the brothel brawl experience? Or had Grandpa not rescued Vani from death and imprisonment so that Sandro would not be an orphan walking the streets alone, unprotected and starving?

Did this God that Dr. Troyer and his Uncle Tony told him about really exist? Did He care about me? Had He orchestrated his life thus far? The "What ifs" swam up and down like a salmon in a rapid stream. Was Cavaliere alive? If so, could Sandro see and comfort him? If his friend was going to die, Sandro wanted to be by his bedside, comforting him. And if he was going to live, Sandro wished to be by his bedside encouraging him. He must go to the hospital and know Giacobbe's status. At that moment, I walked into the room and saw Sandro in shock. The television showed the bombing repeatedly, like the World Trade Towers in New York City on 9/11. Sandro was transfixed and glued to the television screen but held the incandescent candle he got from the young lad. This boy always carried a candle whose wick was always long enough to perpetually be lit, and the wax constantly melting but replenished itself. These miracles of flames are almost like Moses at the burning bush. Why does the little boy always remind the Vitalis to remember?

Although Sandro sat trembling in the dimly lit room, I went to the couch beside my son. I wrapped my arm over Sandro's shoulders. Before I said a word, I imitated the examples of my Grandpa and brother to hold his peace until the grieving Sandro spoke. It took several minutes before either spoke.

Clearing his throat, Sandro cautiously, but with great deliberation, reluctantly explained the story detail after detail of that night, including his experimentation with drugs and sex with his next-door neighbor friend during the last seven months. "Dad, I am sorry it took Cavaliere's injuries to tell you what I have been doing under your nose. I understand how you felt it hard to talk to me about your past and where I came from. Thanks so much for letting me know about all of it. You saved my life again! I love you so much! Had you not told me point by point that I might not be here with you right now! These pieces must fit into a massive puzzle I can't explain."

My eyes dropped a bit in sadness and teared up. I felt a mystical connection and confusion like tides coming in and receding, echoing my past. Pulling myself out of the depression I started slumping into, the present time to care for my son as best I could took precedence. "Let's give the hospital time to handle Giacobbe and others hurt in the blast. I am sure they're super busy, and you'd probably wait a long time to get through on the phone. You can call to find out if he's there in the ICU or something like that. With this type of trauma, ambulances typically go to Saint Andrew's Hospital. Papa told me a little time ago that they are the only hospital with a 'Burn Intensive Care Unit' open to seriously burned patients. You and I should shower, shave, and groom presentable so hospital folk will believe us when we tell the personnel we are Papa's son and grandson. OK?"

"Sure thing, Dad," Sandro breathed a sigh of relief after disclosing what he had been doing with his closest friend. He said nothing about the strange little guy that followed him to the front door. There would be enough time to talk about it later."

They didn't answer the phone at the hospital's ER. But Sandro doggedly kept trying. After he tried several times, I said," Sandro, I know you keep trying to get through to the ER. Call the hospital's operator or dispatcher to get Giacobbe's status. I am sorry you must go through this, Buddy. I am on your side and praying for your friend's recovery. You know, I don't even know how to pray or what for. But your Grandpa has prayed for you all his life, and my little brother, Tony, has too. Despite that, I am trying to pray for Giacobbe blindly. I will leave it up to you to call the "family's experts" like Grandpa or Uncle Tony. If you can ever get a hold of them. They have worked with street people, some of them from the red-light district. So, don't be afraid to tell either of them about this disaster and ask them to pray. They will ask the priests they know and are close to pray for you and Giacobbe confidentially. Do not be ashamed. I am not embarrassed by you but surprised to hear your story. I guess we still need to work on trusting each other. In some ways, it reminds me of when Ken died in my arms about 15 years ago. I will never forget it. Like you and Giacobbe, Ken and I were familiar with finding "red-light districts" anywhere. So, call the hospital operator, then we will go down there in a little while. "

Sandro nodded and replied with gratitude, "Thanks. Dad, I need your help more than ever and support to make it through. Dad.". Sando kept thinking about how kind his Grandpa had been to him and learned all that was happening to him. Additionally, he remembered how special his Uncle Tony was and how he had taken Alessandro under his wings to shield him before.

After calling the operator, it was a relief to hear that Giacobbe was alive; however, he was in critical condition in the burn ICU and on a ventilator. Sandro could text Grandpa and Uncle Tony: "Hi, this is Alessandro. I don't do this often enough, but I ask for your thoughts and prayers for my friend, Giacobbe. He was severely burned and is in critical condition at St. Andrew's Hospital. The hospital wouldn't say he was on life support. But it sounded like he was."

Sandro left his father to get cleaned up from tonight's fiasco and take a long hot shower, thinking about Cavaliere and tonight's divine interruption and intervention, or whatever it was. In a blur, he remembered and retraced the steps he had walked many times before with his friend back to that smoldering building.

He then caught himself thinking like that when Giacobbe was charred, living by artificial means, and shouted aloud, "Giacobbe, why didn't you listen to me!? D*n it! Oh God, have mercy! Who are you, friend, telling me to remember? Tell me! Tell me! I am tired of second-guessing you--you and God!" He then changed the shower's temperature to cold to snap out of where his thoughts were shamefully leading him. He stood in the frigid water with suds all over his body until all he could think about was getting out and drying off. His thoughts were sober; they were intent on seeing his friend and keeping from dying---whatever that would mean. Although his imagination about his addiction mindset was tame now, his perceived adolescent invincibility and omnipotence were blasting in to save his friend.

I was in the kitchen getting some coffee and offered Sandro a cup. He wasn't in the mood. Another thing to cloud his cognition or mess with his feelings wasn't what he needed. He was so wrapped in his thoughts. Sandro was anxious to get on the road to see his pal in the burn unit. Would he be able to stomach viewing his friend and the other scorched bodies or the char enveloping Giacobbe's skin or smell burnt flesh? He was going to try.

Sandro figured putting a lot of deodorant and cologne on he thought would cut down the odor his burnt chum might smell like. So, after several hours, we took off to St. Andrews. I was exhausted from work and, catching myself falling asleep at the wheel, Sandro and I switched places. It would take more hours to get to the hospital safely this late at night, Alessandro thought when it was less than fifteen minutes away.

Then, Sandro saw St. Andrews Hospital because of the slew of ambulances with lights on and flashing. "Dad, wake up! We're here!" the young man squawked out. Sandro kept pushing me to wake up to go inside with him. They stopped and parked abruptly.

Sandro dragged me out of the auto and held my shoulders to walk into the hospital. The Security of the building was skin-tight. The guards blockaded the entrance to avoid having many unknowns and reporters stampeding into that place.

I had finally awakened and explained the situation to Security that they were Dr. Vitali's son and grandson. We knew how to wear protective isolation clothes because Dr. Vitali was one of the global crèmes de la crème infectious disease experts. The guards knew the name of Dr. Vitali and his unblemished reputation, but the Vitalis had to prove their identity before being allowed to enter.

The hospital had a weird scent to it. The smell of fire and carbonized flesh, the smell of alcohol and other hospital cleaning agents. This aroma shocked us as it portended ominous sights ahead. Per hospital infection control protocol, they could only visit one at a time and only for up to 10 minutes each day.

That was totally unacceptable and unreasonable to Sandro. He thought he would need more time than was allotted daily, especially for the young man's invincible powers to prevent Giacobbe's death. Sandro squirmed at the restrictions but conceded that the hospital knew best.

In full hospital PPE, Sandro was first to be let inside. "Oh, my God!" Sandro blurted out but was immediately quelled by the nursing staff. As Sandro got closer, it was apparent that at least 25% of his friend's body was scorched below the skin and, in some places, down to the bone and muscle. He was on a ventilator wrapped in white gauze over much of his body. His face was damaged the most. Giacobbe was almost unrecognizable. Sandro felt nauseous. It was horrifically sad for anyone to see his condition, but the shock and immediate pain it caused was unimaginable for close friends and family. Sandro was crying several feet from the bed. He wished he had kept the one condom between them before the explosion. But even if he did and was the one to keep it, Giacobbe would have gone anyway. The muscleman was dead set on having pleasure that night. Stubborn and obstinate, Sandro's friend found it hard to make him reconsider anything he planned to risk, and fun was not worth the aftermath of these consequences. Parents, priests, and people warned the duo of the possible outcomes; they wanted to protect them from harm. Dire consequences are inescapable from bad choices.

Terrified and shaking again with sobs, the nurses took Sandro out of the area where his buddy had so much denuded skin. The medical team said It would be touch and go for several days if he was to survive.

Sandro overheard the medical staff say that Giocobbe had lost sight, at least in his right eye, and they were not optimistic about his survival, vision, and speaking ability.

Two weeks passed slowly, but Giocobbe gradually came off life support. The long road to being functional would be exasperating and doing therapies painstaking. It was apparent that Sandro's pal's right eye had lost all ability to see, and his left eye could only see through an optic fog due to cornea scarring. To speak, a microphone attached to a tracheostomy (a tube placed in a surgical hole) opening in the throat could communicate with much effort. This man with the once Herculean strength became as thin as a shadow on the wall and the object of scorn and pointing fingers. Following complete facial debridement, he began reconstructive surgeries he had inevitable and repeated reconstructive surgeries. Then, his features were at least tolerable for outsiders to see.

Sandro did help his buddy with therapy and seeing and communicating. Sandro helped him get out of a wheelchair and be his "eyes" for him. Unfortunately, after a while, Sandro grew tired of spending so much time and energy with only minuscule improvement. Alessandro thought "Giocobbe was not my wife and not my sole responsibility. when Sandro could not lose social contact because of him. Chronic illness fatigue had set in, and the distance between Giocobbe and Sandro grew. He wanted liberty even at times the two of them had scheduled. His friend finally gave up on this miserable living and loneliness.

Sandro didn't show at all the last time they were scheduled to get together. He was out drinking with new friends with similar addictions. The day after the "no-show." Giocobbe committed suicide by overdosing on opiates prescribed for his intense physical, social, and emotional pain. He recorded and left a verbal suicide note, which was painfully garbled but mentioned Sandro's name twice distinctly. Giacobbe died that day from lack of medical attention and unbearable social isolation. Sandro was crushed and suicidal, so his Papa returned him to the psychiatric ward. The hospital stay was longer this time, but his Grandpa saw him nearly every other day. But what will happen to Sandro when he's released?

While in the mental health unit, Sando met three Jewish youths, Ari Nephtali, Jeremiah Goldstein, and Myriam Frank; Ari was born and lived in Jerusalem all his life. The others were born in the United States. Jeremiah was raised in Brooklyn, NY, and Myriam grew up across the river in New Jersey. Ari was a practicing Conservative Jew, but the others were not practicing. Myriam and Jeremiah came to Italy from Tel Aviv. The three were brought to the unit to deal with substance use problems. All three plus Sandro had different substance choices (cocaine and hallucinogenic habits, but that is not why they were admitted. There were other reasons than drugs, too.

Ari and Myriam had Major Depressive Disorder. Both attempted suicide from the loss of romantic lovers and the recent deaths of friends and family. Ari hanged himself but was rescued by some random woman and two men. They had never met before. The men and the solitary woman were nameless. The woman vanished soon after the rescue, but the two men called for an ambulance, followed it, made it to the hospital, and stayed with Ari briefly in the ER.

Myriam had purposely overdosed on OxyContin, and her aunt found her limp, prone, and barely breathing with pills scattered on the floor. Immediately, when the medical people saw her, they gave her Narcan. Ari and Myriam required ICU care, many psychotropic medicines, and intense psychotherapy. They appeared to be getting the help they needed.

However, Jeremiah was having daily illusions and distortions of reality. Sandro overheard the doctors diagnosing whether Jeremiah had schizophrenia, substance use, or both.

Only the day Sandro arrived they all sat together through cognitive behavioral group therapy(CBT). "None of this makes sense, and how is this group therapy helping anybody?" was their consensus. During break time, Sandro got to know his new allies. He found out all three had not seen or heard from any of their families in months; Jeremiah had not been with any of his family in two years. During the conversation, Sandro discovered that his Grandpa, uncle, and I contacted him at least every week and sometimes several times per week. He thought about how fortunate he was compared to three new pals.

With the counselors' help, Alessandro realized that his anxiety and depression stemmed from his father; that is to say, he saw my condition gradually deteriorate. My health was slipping away despite all the support from Dr. Rossi. Sandro did not want to see it. The physicians recommended that Sandro talk about it in counseling with me. When the subject was brought up, Sandro just got up from his chair and left the room, bawling secretly and desiring to die first. After a few weeks, Sandro called Grandpa and me to escort him home without protest from any of them. Counselors didn't understand the bond these three generations had for each other.

CHAPTER FOURTEEN:

THINGS FALL APART, AND THE WIDENING GYRE

◇◇

The Second Coming

BY WILLIAM BUTLER YEATS

Turning and turning in the widening gyre
The falcon cannot hear the falconer;
Things fall apart; the center cannot hold;
Mere anarchy is loosed upon the world,
The blood-dimmed tide is loosed, and everywhere
The ceremony of innocence is drowned;
The best lack all conviction, while the worst
They are full of passionate intensity.

Surely some revelation is at hand;
Surely, the Second Coming is at hand.
The Second Coming! Hardly are those words out
When a vast image out of Spiritus Mundi
Troubles my sight: somewhere in the sands of the desert
A shape with a lion's body and the head of a man,
A gaze blank and pitiless as the sun,

Is moving its slow thighs while all about it
Reel shadows of the indignant desert birds.
The darkness drops again, but now I know
That twenty centuries of stony sleep
Were vexed to nightmare by a rocking cradle,
And what rough beast, its hour come round at last,
Slouches towards Bethleham to be born?
n/a
Source: **The Collected Poems of W. B. Yeats (1989)**

Luca could have been a better patient. As a renowned doctor, he had no time for "this thing" called a "heart," as he would refer to it, and made some jokes with friends besides Primo and his family. Primo and the rest of the Vitalis were not amused and took more interest in Luca's heart disease than he did. His family didn't know about the angina every morning, which would sometimes awaken him from sleep.

Luca ate what he wanted without restrictions or recommendations and refused to eat a low salt and fat diet. Traditional Italian mixed with American fast food was his fare. The doctor had no time to count calories, sodium, or saturated fat. However, he recommended it to his patients. He was careful not to show his eating habits in front of Primo and his wife, a well-known cardiologist in Italy. It was like an alcoholic with his bottle of liquor or an addict with a needle and syringe; Luca hid his diet.

Rationally, he knew this was the wrong course of action, But that "physician invincibility." prevailed. He would overwork, overeat, and get little sleep. With this angina aiding his insomnia, his nights of rest were nearly nonexistent.

He started doing medicine's big "NO! NO!": self-prescribing. Not with narcotics, as doctors had. No, this was a bit more scientifically sophisticated. He bought nitrites, specifically amyl nitrite (not nitroglycerin but related), taking some of them from the cardiopulmonary lab but occasionally from some pharmacies that sold them where he could find them, including some out-pharmacy. He was well aware of the positive and negative effects of these drugs. These drugs were legal, but he did not want his family or best friend to worry or be informed about his condition. The positive effects cause blood vessels to relax, which is very helpful in treating angina.

When he took the amyl nitrite "poppers," it would immediately stop the chest pain. However, he also got a "rush." These poppers subconsciously gave him a moment of pleasure as he remembered he had with his wife, Anna-Claire, in days gone by. He felt so lonely for her. He only wanted to be with her again in heaven.

Nevertheless, Luca kept forging away through work and life, especially for Sandro and me. His anxiety was almost always there punching him. Worrying about Alessandro and his suicide attempts I was looking ill. I showed signs of liver failure and was quickly losing weight. My eyes were becoming slightly yellow, as did my skin. With my liver showing more signs of liver impairment, my HIV infection had not had undetectable viral loads for months. Although my T cells were hanging in there and didn't show increasing deterioration. Primo and my father constantly looked at new antiretroviral and anti-hepatitis agents to see if any would show promise in containing my HIV infection.

One of the pharmaceutical firms had recently completed stage III of a new randomized, controlled, blinded clinical trials. Likewise, his liver was beginning to fail, causing jaundice. Sandro lived with each other at some risk of coming in contact with his Dad's blood.

Death was seriously discussed at one family meeting involving Papa, Sandro, and me. "We need to do something that all three of us resolve: what we should do when one of us dies or becomes incapacitated. Concerning me, I don't want to continue the ventilator for more than one week if there is no improvement. Just let me go. 'All my days are written in a book. God has a set time for me to die,' and nothing can thwart His Will. "Papa insisted.

Sandro was shocked by what Grandpa said and rebuked him, roaring and punching the coffee table., "No, Grandpa, no one's dying here. No! NO! Stop talking like that, please. You promised me that if my Dad died, I didn't need to worry about being forgotten. You told me that I could live with you when Dad dies. You said you'd adopt me so I wouldn't be a damn orphan. But if you both are gone, there is no safety for me. No, NO! No one's dying here! No one's going anywhere! NO ONE!"

Dr. Vitali expected what his grandson's reaction would be. He had seen similar responses from patients' families when death was discussed. The denial is woven throughout the human fabric.; speaking about challenging situations seemed to produce the anticipated and natural reaction and refusal of negative news. Luca's voice was firm yet gentle and straightforward yet compassionate. He replied, "Sandro, I am not saying anything about that, I have something to talk to about. The reality is we all die at some end as part of the cycle of nature. We should let our family know what we should decide to do if we get very sick or need to use life support measures or not. Yes, it is about what you want to be done, if you cannot speak for yourself about your decision to be on a ventilator and other supports or not., Fellas, please take me off that way to treat me if there is no improvement over seven days."

I said, "All of you decide whatever you want for my situation." Then Sandro declared, "If Dad dies, I want to be with him, so let me die, and I don't want to be put on life machines."

"OK, guys, keeping these decision cards safe in my secret Papa's jewelry box would be best. now we all know our end-of-life decisions:1) Papa wants to be on life support for no longer than seven days if there is no improvement; (2) I wish to have the family survivors decide; (3) If Vani dies, then Sandro wants to be DNR (Do Not Resuscitate)." Papa declared. "Sandro wants to join his dad in death so he does not want to be put on a ventilator."

"The counselor now at the psych ward and Dr. Troyer impressed on me that I should tell why I keep ending up in the mental health unit. They said, 'Talk with your Dad. He is worried about you. Be blunt but compassionate, about my thoughts and attempts at suicide. In my mind, I am watching you slowly die in front of me, and I can't do a damn thing about it. Not only will I lose you, but I will be alone like an orphan kid.

Sandro continued," As you know, Giacobbe and I frequented the Quartiere a Luci Rosse (red-light district) to get high and have wild sex and orgies with beautiful men and women. We always went together there and scheduled a time to return. While we were hurrying, I wouldn't go to that sleazy place without a condom. We argued about it Giocobbe when I told him how Dad picked up the STDs and that he suffers from those infections. I was not with Giacobbe that night of the explosion. I tried my best to care for Giacobbe after he was burned all over his body. Then later, when I missed watching for him for only one day, he killed himself! After that, his suicide note mentioned my name twice. I could not heal him or make him live without pain. He was following this with a suicide note saying my name twice. I feel so guilty that I wasn't there. But what's bothering me the most is you, Dad. You look like you're dying, and I don't think I can handle that. I love you, Dad, so much; I don't want you to die. We need to find a way to cure you as Grandpapa would." Sandro said solemnly while crouched next to the sofa, sobbing. "You were like me hunting for places to pick up women, booze, and drugs."

I winced about Sandro's remarks. But I looked at my son gently but directly. I was disturbed by his words. Sandro was showered with guilt, shame, and grief. I spoke in muffled tones to his Papa and Alessandro about his fears: fear of death, fear of the pain, especially for Sandro's safekeeping, fear of poverty and unemployment.

"Sandro," Dr. Vitali mildly addressed, "Sandro, I know you are afraid not only of your father's health but also of how you will cope and adjust your life. You are my grandson. I love you very much. You won't be abandoned or orphaned. I will adopt you if you want me to. Don't worry about that. I am always here for you and your Dad."

As soon as Dr. Vitali choked out the words, prophetic words, Luca grabbed his left shoulder and then his chest. He said no words. He dropped to the floor and stopped breathing. I yelled to Sandro to call for an ambulance.

Meanwhile, Uncle Romeo was on a stroll with his two dogs. The dogs had been silent the whole walk until they began barking wildly and pulling Romeo forward. Romeo saw me performing CPR on Papa through the windowpane. He rushed to the locked front entrance and flew to the back door. The dogs followed at his heels, howling loudly. His dogs followed at his heels, barking incessantly. Romeo slammed and burst into the room. Then, Romeo and I continued a more effective resuscitation, and within minutes, the ambulance arrived, and the EMTs carted Luca into it. Then they sped away.

Sandro and I stared blankly with our pupils fully dilated, hearts racing, and bodies trembling as if both were shivering as they had seen a ghost, a phantom., I was dripping with sweat because of resuscitating Papa. I breathed rapidly from the CPR and worried about Papa's low likelihood of survival. He had physically, emotionally, spiritually, and legally saved me from incarceration in a foreign country. Had not Papa come to his side, though disappointed with my situation, I knew I would have been imprisoned and not there for his son.

During the discussion, Sandro, before Papa's collapse, Sandro paced up and down the hallway was constantly plagued that he would be parentless. He thought he would be alone on the street, like Tony's lover, Roberto, dying from viral diseases. I am sure Roberto would have died alone, swept aside, and disposed of like a pound of crap. His Uncle Tony, who now was taking care of Roberto from yesteryear on, was the kindest and the most genuine person he knew. Sandro confided in him because he was listened to and encouraged by his uncle. That was true of all the male relatives he had." What happens to me if Grandpa dies because my Dad is also dying, or at least sicker than I've known all my life."

In desperation, Alessandro called him to inform him of what was happening---Grandpa may be dead, and I was headed down the road. 'Ciao, please let me speak to my uncle, Tony Vitali?"

"My child, do you mean Orazio Vitali? He is in the chapel now. I believe he is praying in the chapel," the aged priest said. "There is an emergency at home!" said Sandro. He was pouring out all his heart to the priest taking the call who had beckoned for someone to get Tony. Roberto was almost mute from anxiety and depression.

Tony was in a perpetual praying and fasting mode, unaware of his family's immediate danger. Tony came to the phone solemnly and said, "Ciao. Is this Alessandro? What is wrong?"

With a quiver in his voice, Sandro told Uncle Tony, "Grandpa held his chest and fell on the ground. Dad and Romeo did CPR on Grandpa while we waited a long time before the ambulance came with EMTs and paramedics. Then, right away, they put a tube down his throat and shocked his chest a couple of times, and then the ambulance rushed down the street with lights flashing and sirens blaring. And it's just Dad and me at home now. Daddy looks like a ghost after giving CPR. Grandpa. I'm so scared. Grandpa is my very close friend. I am so confused and am on pins and needles until we find out if Grandpa made it. He is such a good man. Why should he die, and all the rotten ones remain?"

Calmly and soberly, the monk-to-be conveyed the emotion everywhere and told Sandro, "Let's not jump to conclusions, my dear Alessandro. OK. We all need God to breathe into us freshness. God gives us life and breath and will never desert or abandon us. Let's pray.

Roberto and I will be there in four hours or so. What hospital will he be in?"

While I unapologetically snatched the phone from Sandro's hand, "Hospital of St. Frances of Assisi, we think. Papa said it was the best cardiac hospital in the city. Their intensive care and heart unit was the best." I replied." We will check there first. But it might be the University Hospital close to where Grandpa works. We will be in one of those medical centers."

Roberto looked gaunt and ghastly and had contracted some "viral thing" because he was coughing a lot. Orazio was praying for him and his health. As Tony spoke, clouds outside were merging into a massive thundercloud in Assisi, Milan, and Bologna. It nearly covered all of Northern Italy. This storm was reminiscent of when Dr. Vitali was a boy with a broken bicycle and met Dr. Rossi. becoming lifelong pals.

The rain on the side of the road when a huge thunderstorm followed that hot day so many years ago. It was the time when Luca and Primo connected for the first time. Then, as now, the wind picked up with lightning. The strong winds were gale-like, shipwrecking anything in its path. The storm might take too long to subside.

One of the Franciscan friars brought one of the two reliable automobiles the monastery had. Tony helped Roberto climb into the vehicle. The van looked squirrel-eaten. The former heroin addict slumped in the seat while Tony was helping him into the car; Roberto felt like a skeleton with protruding ribs and nearly every bone on his body. Reaching over Roberto, Tony saw there was no vim and vigor in Roberto's speech or movement. Roberto showed no emotion. It frightened his longtime buddy. Tony sensed he needed to speed as much as possible, which would be challenging and safe during the tempest in this vehicle. The travel time was over three hours from Assisi to Milano, but the storm was furious, and the muscle of rain and hail tried to prevent cars and trucks from moving forward. So, the guys prayed and raced to help the collapsing structure of their household again by disease.

The patriarch, Luca, held our family together from totally collapsing. Throughout his journey on earth, he was not only our biological but a spiritual father. As tears flowed, utter terror consumed both Sandro and me. I was beginning to be unhealthy. Therefore, Sandro encouraged me to lie on the sofa beside him. In acts of tenderness, Sandro let me rest my head on his lap. I was cold but sweating profusely. Then, in a sign of comfort and realizing my future decease may be nearer than he previously thought, Sandro combed my drenched, curly black hair. I was reassured of Sandro's love and concern for me but also pondered what would happen to Sandro if Papa, I, or both of us died soon! With that prospect in mind, I thought Sandro was not well trained to manage life independently and was often suicidal. How does someone prevent a beloved person from dying? How could I interrupt Alessandro from taking his own life before or after my own? What will happen when we breathe our last breath? Is there a set time for every person to be born and a time to die on some eternal universal clock? With each male person in the Vitali family and "Papa's adopted son," Roberto, there were resilient bonds indescribable that yoked them together through thick and thin. They discovered that bonding with each other created courage and supported Vitali's fortress of determination. The covenantal and familial nexus allowed love to flow without fear and doubt to triumph.

In troubled times, Sandro would remember to go and read the Psalm (Ps.139) that both his Uncle Tony and Dr. Troyer directed to him, Psalm 139. Alessandro believed God knew every detail of about me, grandpa, and himself including his time from conception in a brothel to the death of his best friend and drinking buddy. Now, with the two closest family members in jeopardy of losing their lives soon, he was petrified by the future and already feeling grief. It felt unfair. . One of the monks where Tony lived prayed daily with him. Often, they would pray the Lord's prayer, looking to God for wisdom and strength.

CHAPTER THIRTEEN:

STRAWS THAT BREAK THE CAMEL'S BACK

◇◇

Tony tried to keep his eye on the road while the heavy sound of Roberto's ever-increasing crescendo and labored breathing propelled him to drive faster and faster despite the frightful weather. Roberto's cracked lips were blue, his face was ashen sweaty, and his fingertips were cyanotic and cold. Tony and Roberto rarely talked on the trip to the hospital. Tony spoke the most when they did due to Roberto's respiratory fatigue. A coughing spasm accompanied every bump in the road. Unfortunately, there were a lot of them.

Tony told his buddy repeatedly," Roberto, don't worry; we are almost at the hospital. They can care for you better than I do. No one will abandon you. I won't. You won't be alone, my dear one. Papa and Dr. Rossi will give the best care possible. You know I love you. Vani and Papa love you very much, too. I know for sure that Sandro loves and cares about you, too. You'll make it; Hang in there. I know it's tough! Stay in the race." Roberto and Tony made it to St. Francis of Assisi Hospital's Emergency Department in time. Roberto struggled to catch his breath, and the long trip's load robbed him of endurance. Cough after cough with barely a second between each was all he could bear.

Roberto quickly lost consciousness. Had the journey been 10 minutes longer, it would have been fatal.

Tony stopped with keys in the ignition; he flew out of the car and ran into the Emergency Room, yelling, "Hey, there! Hey! My friend is dying. I need someone quick to help us. Quick, I am right outside. Hurry! He's dying! I tell you, he's dying! Please hurry! Come quickly! Help! He's in my car--- get him.," Tony demanded, pointing to the automobile they were traveling in. Tony shouted, "Over here! Over here!"

Roberto was slumped over the seat with his belt in place, holding him from falling forward on the car's floor with its cracks and rust. Tony kept hollering, "Help! Help me! Please, won't someone help me?" Tony, Roberto's lover from his youth, repeatedly saw Roberto's dying and death in this manner, with recurring nightmares with increasing frequency.

He prayed night and day ever since the two of them reconnected. Since I rescued them from Mr. Nicotera's violence and rage many years ago, Roberto's death was constantly on Tony's mind.

A minute seemed like an eternity; the emergency team arrived at the car lickety-split and removed Roberto's seatbelt. When his body almost plummeted to the floor and cement, he was caught by a well-muscled lowly orderly on his second day on the job. The medical staff lifted Roberto onto the stretcher and zoomed into the ER with its well-trained staff. The hospital's ER was particularly busy that night, but the immediacy pushed Roberto briskly onto the examining table with bright lights. The ER anesthesiologist, Ruth Bertolli, and accompanying respiratory therapists (RT), Antonio Mezza Salma and Maria Giordano, quickly and skillfully placed the endotracheal tube (ENT) down his throat. The respiratory therapists used an Ambu bag (bag valve mask) with high-flow oxygen until he was securely on life support and transported him immediately. Multiple IV (intravascular) lines were secured to monitor the function and supply fluids, medications, and blood. He was not an" easy stick" (a person able to have the IV and blood tests drawn without any trouble) because of the multiple sites he used for his IV heroin addiction. He had many scars from drug use and physical trauma, but they found a couple of locations to use.

Within thirty minutes, they stabilized Roberto with IV medicines that raised blood pressure (vasopressors), antibiotics, antivirals, and blood...and on the ventilator. Would Tony ever be able to pray with him again? After they reunited as adult men, their intimacy changed from sexual to spiritual. Tony had been at his side growing up until Roberto's Father's sudden and unexpected death. Then, they were separated. Roberto ended up on the streets, homeless, a "throwaway "---He was a young man without a sense of belonging to anyone. His IV substance disorder was only a symptom of his broken spirit and disenfranchised. His lonely aloofness and feeling of being abandoned by others were prominent. He never had a break. No, No break whatsoever. Except through the Vitali family's generosity and warmth. On top of that, his sexual survival skills got Roberto into many tense, nail-biting moments and multiple poorly treated infections. That was his condition until Tony and he reunited and came under his care and tutelage.

Tony was nearly in a trance while pondering the two of them and his buddy's sorry state. At that moment, Tony was awakened by Aria and me, who had come up to be with Papa but did not know about Roberto's status nor that both were in the same ICU. "Hey Tony, wake up! Wake up!' Then, I shook him into consciousness with a voice of urgency and importance. "Come on, man! Come on, Tony! We've got to talk NOW!"

Tony's eyelids flickered open and sparked him into action and fright and disorientation. "What's happening? Where's Papa? Where's Roberto? Are both still alive? Where are they?" Tony pleaded with rapid-fire questions.

Aria entered the conversation with horror as if viewing a mass grave. "Yeah, Tony. Pray hard and get the abbey to pray right away, OK?"

I interrupted, "Yeah, Tony, I don't know how to pray--like you or Papa do. Our father and Roberto are on vents now. Each of them is hooked up to one. Going through the ER, the whole city will be on one soon. By the way, everyone was coughing their heads off in the ER when Papa came in. Time will tell us what to do, but we've got to get a plan together. A " viral tsunami" is supposed to be coming here within the next few weeks, especially in Northern Italy. I have a terrible feeling about this whole picture. I had briefly heard about this by eavesdropping when Papa was having with Dr. Rossi. A new virus is sweeping through China. Papa said that a virus is innocuous to some and life-threatening to others. It was similar to SARS-CoV-1 in 2002. Only a few countries were affected then. But it has sprawled throughout China, according to Papa and Dr. Rossi a few weeks ago. Already spread to Asian nations nearby, racking up dead bodies as it goes."

"The whole world will be affected and encircled by it somehow by air travel just like it has been forecasted in some books that came up in the last few years," Aria said. "In one of Papa's and my trips to China, he said, 'A person may bring it from one country to another and have multiple layovers in one trip or one day; you can see because that individual could spread another person without knowing it.' Both coronavirus pandemic has started in China, and it's just a matter of time before it will be here in Italy."

"Papa and Roberto have to make it through the night, right?" Tony stated with an emphatic tone. Tony felt he needed to get a breath outside the hospital to get his thoughts centered---to get it together.

Meanwhile, Sandro paced back and forth, shaking his head and mumbling softly incoherent words no one heard. No one listened. something to himself and told the group, "I am going outside to smoke and wrap my head around these last two days." He sounded confused and morose. He walked away from the older adults and moved mechanically down the corridor. The others kept talking without acknowledging his departure. Nobody asked how he was getting along and handling the crises erupting. Frankly, it seemed to Sandro that he was inconsequential and better off dead. He shed no tears, nor did Tony, Aria, or I.

Tony felt overwhelmed by the day. Half of the men he loved the most were at death's doorstep. Tony talked to himself, saying, "Papa has always been God's unique gift to me from the start. Papa understands trauma but routinely opens the door of his life and home to outsiders and prodigals. He is the most godly and fearless person I know. Our father seemed to absorb all life's blows with resolve to make it through for each one of us. I know he took the punches meant for me and the rest of us. With all his heart, Papa sought to understand Tony's and Roberto's relationship. He worked as hard as anyone could for us with some God-gifted charge, talent, and manly character. His middle name should be "Courageous" (Corragiossa). He is an ordinary man with a supernatural love. My hero, Luca Vitali (meaning "light of life").

Roberto and Luca were admitted to the same ICU and only ventilator apart. One by one, the Vitalis paid a visit that night and gave loving words to Luca. But for Roberto, only Tony spent any measurable length of time. Sometimes, other priests would join Tony and pray for him. Tony would always say a prayer with him. Even the nurses seemed stand-offish with Roberto., but Tony remained faithful to the lover of his youth, his friend and "adopted brother." With the same degree of love and affection as Luca loved Anna-Claire, Tony loved Roberto: the same grating of heart existed. Tony was a "Good Samaritan" in taking Roberto under his care when everyone else ignored him.

In the same way, Tony committed himself to stay and pray so no one would die or at least not die alone, mimicking his dad. Fortunately for this couple, Tony was becoming a Franciscan monk, so there was somewhat more leniency for him to see Roberto and his Papa.

Aria, Tony, and I were getting updates from the ICU medical staff when suddenly I remembered that Sandro was not with the family. In fact, I couldn't remember the last time I talked to or saw Sandro. I became panic-stricken and had a cold sweat and cold hands.

"Oh my God, where's Sandro? Where's my son? Shit!! Holy Jesus! I've got to find him! What an imbecile I am!" Shudders and terrors squealed down my spine. "I have got to find him right now! Hey, nurse, could you page my son over the intercom."

"What did you say? Have you lost your son? What is his name? I will get the operator to try to find him," she replied.

"His name is Alessandro Vitali. But he likes to be called Sandro. I insisted. "He is about 180 cm (6 feet) tall. He is buff and has dark, curly hair. He's got a dark complexion and aquamarine-colored eyes. There is a long scar underneath his left shoulder. Ummm…I forgot what he was wearing. Oh no! Probably a white tee shirt and blue jeans with holes. I don't know what else I can tell you. Shit!"

Aria and Tony observed my anxious behavior and attempted to calm me. I would not be comforted--not at all. Aria said in her effort, "Vani, I believe he's OK. I am sure he only tries to hide how hard this is for him." But my eyes teared up, remembering Sandro had tried to take his life thrice before.

Tony aimed to subdue my fears by saying something similar. But Tony only spoke a few words; "God, our Father, direct Vani to Sandro. Let him remember where Sandro goes when he needs space." A thought hit Tony, "Maybe that's what that child with a candle was trying to relate to years ago, Vani."

I remembered where Sandro goes to cool off his temper and lower his emotions. It was the same place I would cool my emotions after Mama and Ken died. Sandro had attempted suicide in that same spot a few times, too. Abruptly leaving my brother and sister, I rushed down the hallway, and like a whirlwind, I made it down the stairs. In a flash, I grabbed my car from the parking lot. Sandro's dad put the "pedal to the metal." Soon. I reached the bridge and stream where Sandro had previously wanted to harm himself. I halted his automobile and quickly climbed out. I looked on both sides of the bridge until I saw Alessandro's clothing on the bank. But I did not see my boy. Alarms went off in my mind, and shivers went down my back. Something was amiss on the bank near Sandro's jeans, and his top lay crumpled in a heap. I ripped his clothes off to swim, if necessary, to swim to find and save my son.

His son was out of my sight. He looked up and down the brook. At last, he could see somebody or something on the opposite side of the stream.

"Hey, Sandro! I am here! Stay where you are. I am sorry. I will come to help." The person looked like Sandro. But oh no! Two men and one woman performed CPR as Romeo and I performed on Papa a day ago. Sandro's dad swam over to the shore as fast as he could. Yes, it was Sandro with gray wrinkled skin, blue lips, and limp with no movement.

I howled, "My son! Oh, my son!! My God! My God!" I fell to my knees on the ground and then prostrated. I sobbed and bawled loudly." God, don't take my child. I will give you all of me. Save him! Save me! Please, please! I will do anything, but don't let my only son die! I beg You! "I cried and pled out repeatedly. He heard my pleas echo back, and I remembered a song I had heard from the musical *Les Misérables* stage performance years ago when Papa took Sandro and me to see it in Milan. I was being tortured with my father in critical care on a ventilator and whether my only child, my only son, was dead or dying at the same time before my eyes. How much more tragedy must I carry on my feeble back! I was being macerated bit by bit. Everything is beyond hope! Absolutely impossible to change!

Bring Him Peace, Bring Him Joy

Most blessed One, Holy God
Ancient of Days, Generous Lord
Hear my prayer
In my need
You have always been there

Bring him peace
Bring him joy
Bring him life
He is only a boy

My son is so young
He's shaking in fear

Let him rest, loving God
Soften Your cruel blows
Let him be Heaven blessed

Bring him home
with a heart full of song
Raise him up
Bring him home
the son I came to know
You granted me a son
winter frost came too quickly
cold clouds run to block the sun

How soon they fly
How soon the flower withers
How soon the bloom fades

Soon and very soon
I am old
And will be gone
You can take
You can give

Bring him home
Bring him hope
the's too young to take flight
He is only a boy

You can take
You can give
God, no farewells
Let him live

Bring him home
Bring him a song
before he flies in the skies
Bring him home
Bradford Gilmore (AgapePhileoEros) 2023

(loosely inspired by "Bring Him Home" from the stage production *Les Misérables* by Songwriters Alain Albert Boubul, Claude-Michel Schonberg, and Herbert Kretzmer)

As I bawled uncontrollably, I felt a warm hand on my head. I shifted my gaze and saw the same phantom who would always come at our times of greatest need. Also, there was that same little lad with his candle softly singing. I gazed at this entity, this ghost; I felt this person as close as family. Could it be Dr. Troyer, the psychiatrist Sandro saw on his first psychiatric hospitalization? She looked vaguely the same. Could it be my mother? Now, and at times like this, I felt the same warmth, communion, and care growing up from Anna-Claire before she passed away. Could that little guy be my brother, who had died at birth? Guiseppe? Who, I had heard only a smattering of remarks through the years? That death forever changed my parents, especially my mother, from being a gung-ho, die-hard career-seeking woman to content."

She brought Good News. "Your son will live. He is breathing on his own and has a pulse now. He needs to be handled gently and carefully. He needs a neck metal collar to hold his head in place. The ambulance shouldn't be too long. He was in the water briefly but must have swallowed and inhaled a lot of brook water."

The EMTs and the whole ambulance crew, with Sandro, got him on a stretcher and into the ambulance gingerly. The vehicle traveled on the smoothest road and no bumps in the way. I wanted my boy to go to where his grandfather and Sandro's" adopted" uncle were on ventilators.

The family has been exposed to COVID-19 in the hospital, as well as Roberto and Dr. Vitali, I felt that I was a curse on his family. I could not understand any other reason for me being in some significant role in all my family's woes. I was always part of all the crises my family faced---sometimes the villain, sometimes the victim, sometimes the vulnerable and curse subjecting the family to fates on ventilators.

I pondered, "What would I do if I needed a ventilator? Would we take Roberto off first? Surely, we should care about his situation. Roberto was gay, homeless, substance' abuser, abused, and sick but had never had a fair chance to live humanly and humanely except in Vitali's home care. Would Roberto possibly give up his ventilator for someone else "more deserving?"

"Would one of us give up our position if we became so ill we needed a ventilator to keep Papa on the ventilator?" That was the question all of us were thinking. Although not scripted, Papa told his friends and us to take him off support for another who needed life support if there was no improvement in his condition after seven days. Should we honor that or keep him on to spare his life? He has been at the center of and helped us and many others throughout the years? Can we dare lose his ability, persistence, and devotion to cure diseases during this and future pandemics? Whether he is getting off the ventilator for someone to save another's life or to remain active and help Italy and the changing world during this new pandemic? Would it be selfish of us to take him off at all?" Tony questioned. "That would be the biggest horror and saddest day of my life! But if he was not taken off and a member of our family, including Roberto, needed the last ventilator, it would kill him to know his ventilator could have saved our lives and those of others outside the family. It would kill his spirit and character of compassion and love that we all want to emulate."

"Should we consider Alessandro on a ventilator to keep him on life support, though he had attempted suicide four times? He's young; the doctors think he has a traumatic brain injury or spinal cord damage that could lead to paralysis. Who would take of him since you're getting sicker by the day? Sorry to bring that up, but you have gotten sicker almost daily. In the last year, Vani, but how paralyzed would he be? We all love Alessandro deeply, too. It is unbearable to think of him dying; it has ripped my heart out with every attempt to take his own life! In the last couple of years, to see him want death so much, but maybe he would give that up if he saw that everyone in the family cared for him like you do," Aria asked. "Sandro's deepest fear is to lose you, Vani, or ever become an orphan. Papa said he would step in and be there for him, but Papa's on the vent, and Roberto's enormous challenges in life are known to Sandro-- the nitty-gritty. It would be the continual state of being lost, alone, disabled, and abandoned."

"Should I be alive and my son dying without a ventilator? That is unconscionable. It's not even on the table! It is not on the table! Hear me! But who would care for my son if or when I get too sick and he attempts suicide again?" Vani exclaimed." No! That would kill me, too! This is too much for me to handle. This is so confusing…so confusing!"

This discussion was on everybody's mind. Anna-Claire's and Giuseppe's deaths frequently opened up the subject of human mortality and immortality. The stark reality of the family's vulnerability was staring them smackdab in the face. Who in Italy would be the last person to be put on a ventilator and empty up that life-support for another was not just the Vilalis' question. Still, every Italian had to confront in person or through relationships as Italy sharply submerged under the weight of mass infection, lack of ventilators, lack of PPE, but probably the most significant was the dearth of doctors, nurses, frontline medical and emergency personnel plus farmers and their co-laborers.

"What should we do? Let's call Dr. Rossi. He'll know what to do. He knows medicine and all of us well, especially Papa," Aria brainstormed and was without any further suggestions. Aria and Tony agreed, saying in unison." I will call him right now! "They tried calling, and all his messages went directly to voicemail. Aria and Tony texted his phone and are still awaiting a response. He must be tied up with all this awful viral stuff.

"Of course, Dr. Rossi and Dr. Vitali are the nation's hope for remedy and survival. We knew that Papa couldn't take action on public health strategies. We couldn't ask a person on a ventilator life and death decision, especially of his own family. Where was Primo coming to save the day?" Aria questioned.

At the same time, Dr. Rossi was under stress to both examine and treat the patients and fill in for Papa's absence. He had to designate a few younger doctors and scientists, which was taxing. Replicas are handy when you need them, but in crises like COVID-19, there's nothing like the real thing. Besides that, Papa ran Italy's most prestigious virologic lab. Less experienced and creative scientists became the director of it, but would that be enough?"

Dr. Rossi was six years older than their father and is thought to be in excellent physical and mental health. With increasing age comes slower abilities to think and play with sleep and the circadian rhythm indicators of stress. He covered three hospitals without his partner's buoyancy and intellect to keep him afloat in this overwhelming crisis. He has been working nonstop for days.

Luca (Dr. Vitali) showed no improvement after being on the ventilator. Teamwork, even with some disability, would be better than no one. Roberto began showing some signs that he could come off life-support.

In a trance, Vani remembered the mysterious woman, a female benevolent phantom, rescuing Sandro from two of his suicide attempts, bringing him to the mental health unit next to where Dr. Vitali worked---also, the current one some trauma with Vani's son who was found in the river. The family thought he'd "completed" the suicide itself. Tony didn't believe Sandro was trying to end his life. He was saved and brought to shore by two unidentified men who did CPR before the ambulance arrived—the head injuries on his face around the back to his spine. Tony claimed, "Sandro had removed his dirty clothes to skinny-dip (nude swimming) in a small inland sea. Tony blurted out emphatically, "Sandro will get through this for a better life. Something happened to him and not by his own hand." We disagreed with Tony's opinion but not maliciously and with respect and consideration.

Luca's cousin and support, Anita, spoke, "The Director of Health said they had discovered the virus that people daily cases were dying from right and left, and quarantine enforced. Washing hands, mask-wearing, standing about six feet apart, and inflexible orders: Quarantine. Quarantines blocking international airports, shutting down jobs, most of the tourist economy changing hospitalization visitation strict rules must wear masks wherever you go. We know the virus that caused this epidemic is caused by a virus closely related to SARS. SARS-1 had a high mortality rate but in only a few nations. "

Aria stated, “I have been to China with Papa and Primo. There is where they say the coronavirus originated, and that country took extreme measures of quarantining those who had it and those who were exposed. I heard they even tied one of them to a tree that was not cooperating. Let’s hope that none of us get it!”

Shortages of nurses and doctors and no ventilators in reserve plummeted Italy into despair. The morale of the first responders got lower and lower with each passing day. The Vitali family was in agony, worried, and fearing what the following days, weeks, and months would bring. The hope for instant miraculous intervention was fading fast. It appeared that Tony had hope and faith that miracles could happen for the best among the rest of the Vitalis’ dread and gloom.

CHAPTER FOURTEEN:

ACROSS THE GREAT DIVIDE

◇◇

Then, some of the saddest news of the day came from the doctors caring for Alessandro. Dr. Angelo San Filipo, Dr. Bernadette Bahkita, and Dr. Primo Rossi walked toward the Vitali family. They told them about Sandro's deteriorating prospects of living and, with some certainty, that his recovering unscathed neurologically was only a distant chance. Initially, the Vitali clan lit up as they saw Dr. Rossi, whom they had tried to reach for advice about the prospects of all their loved ones in the ICU.

Primo took a deep breath and hesitantly began talking to the family he knew so well. "Hello, everyone. These are some of my colleagues: Dr. San Filippo, a neurologist, and Dr. Bernadette Bahkita, a neurosurgeon, among the top specialists in the country. Your father and I have worked alongside them for many years." then, looking at the floor, he said, "I have some terrible news; unfortunately, we have to discuss..." his voice trailed off and became inaudible to all the family. Then he patted Dr. San Filippo on the shoulder to talk as he moved away from the family's view.

The neurologist came forward and spoke straightforwardly with directness and compassion. "I am very sorry to inform you that the MRI scan of Sandro's brain shows bleeding and swelling that unless we intervene surgically, Sandro will most likely die, and if he survives, he may be paralyzed, in a coma, or live with a closed head traumatic brain injury. No matter what, he will require special vigilance and care for the rest of his life. It appears Sandro had taken some edible cannabis laced with LSD and probably got disoriented when he was swimming and got tired. It looks like he hit a rock and became unconscious. Lucky for him, somehow, someone found him in time. At least, right now, he is alive."

My face burned red, and I started yelling at all three doctors in rage and panic. "No, he is not going to die! She said so! No, no, no! My boy won't die! I am sure of it!" Unthinking and agitated, I almost physically attacked the people I needed the most if Sandro was to survive. Immediately, Romeo and Tony grabbed me to hold me back.

At that juncture, I felt that same warm invisible hand and presence from the same benevolent person from the shore who was with the men working to save Sandro's life and spoke to him. This soft voice said, "Your son will live. Don't be afraid. Everything is possible for those who believe. For man, this is impossible. But for God, nothing is impossible."

I heard that voice repeatedly like an echo. Romeo and Tony felt a breath and cleansing comfort but discerned no voice. A holy hush and calm that they had never known but always had known changed anger into a bit of hope and trust. All three looked at each other and said not a word.

Dr. Bakhita, an Italian African woman, said impatiently but with genuine care, "I am so sorry, but time is running out. We must act now while we have this narrow window of time to get him to the operating room. She handed Vani a clipboard and form. "Do you consent to neurosurgery on your son, Alessandro Vitali, to relieve the brain pressure and stop the bleeding there? There are possibilities of more bleeding, infection, permanent vegetative state, nerve damage, and death. These are not small risks, but we hope to be lifesaving."

Quickly, I agreed and signed it. Immediately, the medical staff prepared Sandro for neurosurgery and whisked him off to the Operating room. Tears rolled down all of the family's faces and Dr. Rossi's. But in a short time, he regained his composure.

"You all said you needed my help. How else can I help you? You had questions about your Papa and Roberto. What do you want me to know or do?" Primo asked as only a friend could. He rubbed his forehead, sweating intensely, and squinted his eyes. "Man, do I have a headache!" Let me get some water. I have a little tickle in my throat. I am going to lie down for. An hour or so. Then, I will be back." He pulled away from the family and sat in the doctor's suite. He drank a tall glass of cool water and took some acetaminophen. He laid down on the bed where he had been sleeping for the last week before rising to take care of his caseload and Luca's. Before he closed his eyes, he heard reports of spiraling death counts, including prominent Italian physicians. Yet, out of evident exhaustion, he collapsed into sleep.

Those non-admitted Vitali clan members emerged from the hospital. Vitali's family huddled in a friend's apartment to determine the next step. To their surprise, Roberto's respiratory and liver tests showed improvement. Maybe in the next 24 hours, he could come off the ventilator! Papa's state was stable but stagnant. Everyone was agonizingly tired, but the most worrisome was me. I said I felt feverish, but probably all the events were taking their toll on me. I drifted off to sleep in the comfort of Tony's lap and curled up against my brother's Franciscan frock.

Several years ago, I had a similar dream of finding Ken's body cold as ice, motionless, slumped against the bar where they used to get drunk, and sometimes brawl with the fascist element in London while studying at Oxford. And like before, Ken's wound was bleeding, flooding the pub into the streets like the ocean where they swam. But more clearly than before, I saw Sandro on a ventilator. In fact, I was viewing my son's condition up close. Also, I saw myself coughing up blood and the doctor ramming that damn tube down my throat.

I awoke with choking and hacking. My gasping caught Tony off guard, who was silently praying while stroking my drenched hair. I was ill with a fever of 39 degrees Celsius (102.2 degrees Fahrenheit), hacking up blood. The persisting cough couldn't be stopped.

"Vani, we've got to get you to the ER! Pronto!" Tony insisted. The small group sponged me off from top to bottom, got me dressed, and skirted me off, mask and all, to the Emergency Room, packed to the gills with the coughing and sneezing populace. While most wore face coverings, others had thrown them on the floor because of breathlessness. Most were struggling to catch their breath and grab the attention of the medical staff to the point of clutching the men and women in white PPE (Personal Protective Equipment) to drag them into the crowd. PPE was scarce enough in Italy, as were the needed personnel. The tension in the room was palpable and peaked with each additional patient. Some were there with other horrendous medical conditions. Two patients died from cardiac arrest amidst the chaos, and the room was full of face-to-face contact. No social distancing was possible or could be enforced. Pure mayhem!!

Through it all, Tony kept calm and focused on eternity, sometimes Armageddon, and sometimes on Christ's return. He kept rehearsing to trust that even his small faith could do immense work. Tony sent the rest of the kin back to the small apartment where they had been. But Romeo would not leave with Aria and Anita. Neither Tony nor Romeo could leave anyone behind, just like was etched in our father's persona. The crowd thinned a bit. Finally, they called for Giovanni Vitali. By then, I was drenched. My respiratory fatigue put me in earthly peril.

Tony waved and yelled, "Over here." Then Romeo and Tony lugged me to be examined. I was nearly dead weight. The doctor who aided my mother, Anna-Claire, in the emergency room and got her to the obstetrical OR to deliver Tony in decades past came out of retirement to help with the uproar in the ER. Dr. Nicolas DeLorenzo was there and saw the Vitali trio through the mob. By then, I was utterly speechless and running low on respiratory reserve. Immediately, the doctor got me on 30% high-flow oxygen and BiPAP to keep me breathing while waiting for a room and possibly a ventilator.

At that point, Dr. Rossi and I each needed life-support measures to remain alive. Primo was now in his 70s, and I had not been responding to my latest HIV medications. It was planned to switch me to a new drug that could cure HIV and COVID-19. Neither was an optimal candidate for treatment in the ICU. Only one ventilator was left in Italy. The only one happened to be in the same hospital as Roberto, Luca, and Sandro. The only one who was improving was Roberto. But the need was urgent for him to open a ventilator; Primo or I could die within only a few hours. That would jeopardize Sandro's hope for long-term care if Sandro survives; likewise, if Dr. Rossi should succumb to COVID-19, the loss of his medical brilliance, experience, and governance of Italy's public healthcare crises would be lost

CHAPTER FIFTEEN:

GUARDIAN ANGELS OR WHAT?

Although Roberto's condition improved, it took hours to successfully wean him off life support. With as much PPE as possible, Tony rounded on his family, going from bed to bed, anointing them with oil while he prayed and fasted for them. This time, his brother, nephew, Papa, beloved friend, and Dr. Rossi were in trouble. When Tony reached the ICU, Roberto looked the best he had seen for months. He had his eyes open but could not speak.

This day, the priest-to-be, Tony, came to Roberto's bedside to pray for him as he had done countless times before. Roberto's color had changed. to a bit pinker with a yellow tint due to jaundice from his Hepatitis B and C. But Tony noticed something different. It was obvious. Tony believed some miraculous intervention might be afoot. The atmosphere seemed different around his friend. Not a physical one, but a positive spiritual climate change.was happening. It was something like hope, but maybe Tony was deluded or hallucinating. No matter what it was, it was real!

The doctors and nurses began to wean Roberto from the ventilator and decreased his sedation. This young man he had brought from the monastery to the Emergency Room on that blustery, hellish, soggy day, constantly coughing and almost unconscious from his lack of oxygen, was finally improving! Additionally, he showed some animation and movement.

The physicians were rounding on their ICU patients with dread and depletion and went bedside to bedside robotically. The hoary-haired gentleman who was the attending physician (who had seen it all) squinted to make sure he was correct by looking at Roberto and his chart. A week or so earlier, he was ready to pull Roberto off for "more deserving" patients, mainly his colleagues struggling with COVID-19. He appeared baffled by the stark improvement of Roberto over only 24 hours.

The older man was one of Primo's and Luca's most cherished and devoted friends and allies. His name was Dr. Mattio Fontana, and he was Italy's cleverest intensive care and pulmonology expert since the HIV/AIDS and COVID-19 pandemics began. He was one of the physicians who cared for Anna-Claire after Tony was born decades ago. He was one of the pallbearers who carried Anna-Claire's coffin to the grave. Although he was among the intellectual elite at the hospital, he was humble and soft-spoken. He was even more so after many patients succumbed to this "novel coronavirus."

He approached Tony, who was praying with his eyes shut, and uttered hesitantly and respectfully, "Excuse me, sir. I am sorry, Father, but are you Dr. Vitali's son? Are you Tony Vitali?"

The question startled the youthful monk, "Why, yes, sir, I am. How do you know who I am?" Tony replied. "I've never been called "Father" by anyone before. Are you one of my Papa's associates? I am afraid I don't recognize you. However, your voice sounds familiar. Who are you, if I may ask?"

With a smile and half-cheerfully, the elderly gentleman said, "I am one of your father's friends. I knew your mother before her death. You were very young and distraught then, so you probably don't remember me. I have worked practically side-by-side ever since with your Papa." Pointing to Roberto, "Is he your friend? You seem particularly fond of him. The nurses told me about him and that you have come by praying for all of your family and him daily. I have been so concerned since so many of your family are in the unit." With compassionate eyes like Papa's, it was as if he saw your soul. That feeling was most needful now. Just some words of concern lightened the yoke of fear and heaviness. Just to be seen, acknowledged, and heard stirred Roberto's faith and Tony's hope and love for all the family and friends in this critical hour.

Upon hearing the conversation, Roberto's ears pricked up. He started motioning for both of them to come closer, which they did. It seemed apparent to the doctor and Tony that Roberto wanted to come off any further life-support measures. Since his dramatic improvement and the urgency of the need for others to be on the vent, although the specialist and Roberto's best friend were skeptical and reluctant to do so, Dr. Fontana and Orazio believed the time was still too soon to pull this immunocompromised and chronically ill patient off the machine which had kept him going for weeks; nevertheless, they consented to do so. They took him off safely, and he only needed BiPAP and high-flow oxygen briefly. Then, the ICU nearly broke into song and applause at Roberto's bravery and successful redemption of health.

Roberto was still frail; it was evident he was excited and happy to be free of it. Of course, his voice was very coarse and uneasy to understand. He did get a tracheostomy eventually. He said, "Let me be a hero at least once in my life! I want to make room for Vani to get this respiratory support. Vani saved my life. I want to rescue his."

Shaken a bit by the request, Dr. Fontana was faced with the nightmarish decision, which lamentingly was all too common for him. Now, he was faced with a pick between Roberto's request for me or the life of his best and closest comrade, Primo. Primo and Luca were Mattia's best friends for over a quarter of a century; Primo was the oldest at 72 years and had been the stabilizing rock everyone turned to when distressed. Now, he was the country's biggest hope.

Dr. Rossi's and my needs were increasingly severe, but Tony and Dr. Fontana broached the matter with both men. Although Dr. Rossi's situation was dire, he wanted his best friend and me to go on living. If Primo could prevent the death of any of Vitali's family, Dr. Rossi would surrender his life for theirs. He had heard someone once say," Greater love has no man than this than he lay down his life for his friends."(John 15:12-13). He had heard it one time as a boy. No. He heard it from Luca before Anna-Claire and the rest of the family attended a Good Friday Mass after she was released from the hospital following Tony's birth. This time, "the rubber hit the road." Whether or not Primo converted to Christianity before he died self-sacrificially is unknown, yet he followed Jesus in love and chose not to save his own skin but gave up his life for me and others

Luca remained in critical condition on life support with no apparent improvement. He had others swear to take him off the lifegiving support if there was no status change after one week. He repeatedly asked that before he was put in the ICU. It had been going on for several weeks, and his bidding needed to be heeded. How long would the physician's convalescence be when discharged from Intensive Care? He could not take on the load Primo had been carrying nor the country's woes. Could Dr. Rossi or Dr. Vitali function in any of their previous capacities and continue to be healthy if they would pull through? The Italian medical landscape was becoming more and more barren. Many hospital personnel, doctors, and nurses either were COVID-19 positive and in quarantine or were ill or had succumbed to the COVID-19 plague. Some could not tolerate the load or the melancholy pervading each hospital, especially those whose colleagues died; the path ahead was foggy, soggy, and had readied itself for the snares and calamitous avalanche to come.

Joyfully, Sandro made it through surgery successfully but was not safely out of the woods. But still required hyperventilation, mannitol, and phenobarbital-induced coma for a bit longer. It still was unknown what his neurologic sequelae might be if he could remain alive. If I didn't make it, who would take of Sandro, who had already attempted suicide repeatedly when I was still alive? Maybe not this last time, but Sandro obviously had some deep-seated mental health issues, including a substance use disorder, anxiety, and depression, especially around the prospect of his Dad dying. If I passed away and Sandro's ventilatory support could have kept his dad alive, what kind of person would he perceive himself to be? Wouldn't Sandro blame himself as the young man had done all his life for his father's other illnesses? Would he be an orphan as he often feared if I did not survive? Would he end up as a homeless street kid?

Meanwhile, I was not able to think clearly. Would I be responsible or blamed for yet another death in my lifetime? Am I a villain? I have been accused of the murder of my best friend, Ken, and causing Roberto's dad years ago to perish while rescuing Tony and Roberto.

Like Papa, Primo demonstrated sincere courage and loyalty with genuine love by saving his best friend, the stranded youth, from mounting storms to rescue me from peril. Dr. Rossi was a diamond among men. Regardless, the doctor insisted and granted life support to me. Tony prayed with him and gave his last rites. Nonetheless, Dr. Primo Rossi maintained his laudable respect and dignity until he died two days later.

Likewise, Roberto took the uncertainty of what would happen to him being taken off the ventilator.

I was put on the ventilator that Roberto had been on immediately when it became available. It shifts you to a new and surreal perspective on life. I was powerless to help Sandro or advocate for him—it was not in a position a father would ever want. To be impotent is more than sexual. When you can't stand up for someone you love, your failure hits you in the gut, and you are embarrassed, mad, and deflated. My eyes searched and searched for Sandro but could not tell whether he was doing well or still on the ventilator. I was on the ventilator for over a week and made a slow but steady process.

"Vani, this is Dr. Fontana. You are making good progress, and hopefully, we will get you out of the ICU very soon. I wanted to let you know that Sandro is off the ventilator today. He is alert and conversant, but unfortunately, he is paraplegic. Despite Sandro's paralysis, he says he is very grateful for life and new life, but I am sure he will require psychiatric and psychological care for a long time. Sandro contacted a few groups like Alcoholic Anomalous and Narcotics Anomalous. Also, he has been talking on Zoom to priests who counsel him. He says he is now determined to live and committed to remaining sober. Your brother, Tony, is teaching him the Bible, and he says he is planning and willing to attend Mass, at least when Tony goes with him for Christmas, New Year, and the day the Patron Saint of Italy is celebrated. (October 4, the St. Francis of Assisi Day.) Other people care for him and meet his needs with a nutritious diet, physical therapist workouts, prayer and counsel, and social and family support. Every morning since he came off the ventilator, Sandro prays with Tony for you, your family and friends, Italy, and the world."

The week Primo died, Sandro was able to come off ventilatory support. Over the next three and one-half months, he grew more robust but still required a lot of assistance and the use of the wheelchair. He needed physical therapy because he was so deconditioned from his time on the ventilator. His nutrition was important in his healing. Anita or Aria composed and administered high protein and no added salt diets. His intellect was not impaired despite the shipwreck and rocky journey he had been on. He entered an online university-based Information Technology (IT) program six months after discharge. Although Sandro, like all of us, had good and bad days, productive and idle days, he was grateful, and his mood and substance disorder were well-controlled. No more talk of being a "bastard" or an "orphan."

Excitedly, Sandro came in alone and prayed for Papa to stably come off life support. Amazingly, about four hours later, Papa's need for the ventilator was greatly diminished, showing a turnaround of events! Three days later, he was able to be removed from the device. He hated and was frustrated with having a tracheotomy and his need to have it.

Yet, like he had always done in the past, Luca walked again through stormy seas and became triumphant.

I was the last to go on the ventilator and the last to come off, but I had a shorter course than anyone in the family. I felt weirdly alone when I became the only Vitali remaining on the machine. However, one week after Papa was disconnected and discharged home, Sandro, Tony, and Papa visited and prayed with me there.

"Vani, whether you believe it or not, you have been the tissue, the glue, holding us together for decades. Unfortunately, you witnessed great pain, worry, doubting, and sorrow. I know you cannot continue being our "Rock." It is too stressful. You can no longer be the fulcrum of blame, agony, and desperation. You are not a curse to us, either! You are not alone in this world and will not be forgotten. I love you, Vani. Thank you! We want you to come home very soon," Papa declared. After he spoke to me, my progress improved rapidly. Besides coming off the ventilator successfully, one of the pharmaceutical companies came out with a new antiretroviral medication that had properties against all three viruses (HIV/AIDS, hepatitis C, and SARS-CoV-2 or COVID-19.) My depression and Sandro's has been abating. There is no more hiding between us; we have a bright future if we cherish every day as we did when we were taken off artificial life support.

I can't begin to think I am a "Rock" or mortar between family members. No, I am sure that fits Papa better. He who has been there for all of us despite his hectic schedules and the lack of an in-the-flesh intimate partner to shoulder the weight of raising children, children who have faced true life and death battles against dismal odds into triumphs. He saw us through until the war was won! He is an example of courage, strength, and humbleness. I am so grateful to have him as my Papa and hope I can walk worthy of being his son. I want to be like that for Sandro.

Two years following Roberto's release from the hospital, he died peacefully in the arms of his beloved Praying Priest, Orazio Antonio Vitali; both of them lived and served in the abbey in Assisi following Roberto's miraculous survival off the ventilator of COVID-19. The wondrous hospital discharge of the Vitali clan during that horrifying nightmarish onset of the COVID-19 pandemic in 2020.

When You Walk Through a Storm

When you walk through a storm
Hold your head up high
And don't be afraid of the dark
At the end of the storm there is a golden sky
And the sweet silver song of the lark

Walk on through the wind
Walk on through the rain
Though your dreams be tossed and blown
Walk on, walk on, with hope in your heart
And you'll never walk alone
You'll never walk alone

When you walk through a storm
Hold your head up high
And don't be afraid of the dark
At the end of the storm there is a golden sky
And the sweet silver song of the lark

Walk on through the wind
Walk on through the rain
Though your dreams be tossed and blown
Walk on, walk on, with hope in your heart
And you'll never walk alone
You'll never walk alone

Walk on, walk on, with hope in your heart
And you'll never walk alone
You'll never walk, you'll never walk alone

Source: Musixmatch
Songwriters: Oscar Hammnerstein and Richard Rodgers

www.ingramcontent.com/pod-product-compliance
Lightning Source LLC
Chambersburg PA
CBHW071608030726
47593CB00001BA/365

* 9 7 8 1 6 3 8 1 2 8 2 9 8 *